C000065902

CF

Also available from Headline MAN2MAN

Crossing The Line

Anthony Crowther

Copyright © Anthony Crowther 1999

The right of Anthony Crowther to be identified as the Author
of the Work has been asserted by him in accordance with
the Copyright, Designs and Patents Act 1988.

First published in 1999
by HEADLINE BOOK PUBLISHING

A HEADLINE MAN2MAN paperback

10 9 8 7 6 5 4 3 2 1

ISBN 0 7472 6098 2

Typeset by CBS, Martlesham Heath, Ipswich, Suffolk
Printed and bound in Great Britain by
Mackays of Chatham PLC, Chatham, Kent

HEADLINE BOOK PUBLISHING
A division of Hodder Headline PLC
338 Euston Road
London NW1 3BH

Thanks to Tony for encouragement, James for inspiration, and my family for more than I deserve

Chapter One

MIKE

It had been a good week so I decided to take the night off for a change. It was still Saturday night, however, so I went out on the circuit anyway. You'd expect someone like me to spend his entire evening socialising when I'm on the scene, having met nearly everyone in some form of professional capacity or other. That's far from the truth. Most ex-punters don't want to be seen with you for fear of being identified as punters, so that rules out one group of social connections. The second consists of other professionals. As a rule, they're looking for work if you see them out on the scene and wouldn't thank you for wasting their time talking to them and making them look unavailable. The third group are strangers. And you don't get many of them at my age.

Given all of that, you may wonder why I bother going out at all when I'm not working. The truth is that I'd go mental if I spent all my time staring at the same four walls of my flat. Oh sure, there are other things to do, but I haven't got a telly and I hate doing other things (cinema, theatre, etc.) by myself, even if I could afford them. I suppose those are the two main reasons I got into this job. Money and loneliness. But that's another story.

Anyway, I still enjoy going to the clubs, even when I'm not looking for business. I like the music, you see. Okay, it's also a bit of an ego boost. I look after myself. I have to or I wouldn't get any decent clients, just the no-hopers. So when I get all kitted out for a night on the town I get quite a few appreciative glances parading around the club and showing off on the dance floor. Not that anyone does anything more than look. You see, all the nights spent with clients coupled with all the nights spent alone tend to make you hard. If you're not, you don't cope. It all shows through as an attitude.

This all means that it's something special when someone shows enough interest to make a move on me when I'm out and not working. At least it starts out special.

I'd noticed this guy staring at me while I was on the dance floor so I decided to give him a bit of a show. I'm not particularly reserved with my dancing anyway, but this time I made sure to flex and shake to the best effect. Oh, I played it cool, no shared looks or flirty glances, I wouldn't want him getting the wrong idea. I just kept my best points in his line of view. After a while I got bored with giving him a cheap thrill and figured I could do with a drink, so I sauntered across to the bar. This was when he made his move.

'You must be shattered after all that dancing,' he says with his mouth about as close to my ear as he could get without breathing down it. Anyway I figured he was harmless, and I'm usually a good judge of character – you have to be in my business – so I play up to him a bit more.

'Too right,' I reply and dump my head on his shoulder as if I need a nap. So he freezes. The poor guy must have panicked. You could feel the tension in his entire body, so I moved before he was in danger of doing himself an injury. He still looked flustered, but was obviously trying not to show it as he offered to buy me a drink. That usually leads to complications so I was

2

glad I'd already ordered my own. He looked so dejected when I told him no that it was painful. The earlier tension just drained from him and his whole body sagged. I really felt sorry for him. So I handed him my glass and asked him to look after it while I went to the loo. I left him with quite a smile on his face.

At that point I wasn't sure whether I was going to just leave him there or not, but then I bumped into Terry.

Terry was a former punter who wouldn't let go. I'd been with him once, and he declared his undying love for me as he lay basking in the afterglow of a 'too-quick' orgasm and I tried to clean up and get away from him just as quickly. I'd done my best to avoid him since then. Telling him I was busy every time he phoned didn't make much difference so I started agreeing to meet him and not turning up. Eventually he took the hint.

This night he decided to try again. He tugged at my arm as I came out of the loo. When I realised it was him I gave him my iciest stare, but he was immune to anything short of physical violence. And believe me I'd been tempted by that quite a few times. I told him I wasn't working that night, but he just joked about getting a 'freebie'. I tell you, I was so close to punching his lights out that I had to get away fast. I told him I'd seen a friend and managed to lose him in the crowd between the loo and the dance floor. It wasn't easy, believe me, I had to keep swerving between people and doubling back on myself. So I was relieved to see the other guy still waiting by the bar with my drink.

He must have been about ready to give up on me as he nearly jumped out of his skin when I spoke to him. I could see Terry still watching, so I made a big show of being pleased to see the other guy and started chatting as if we were long lost pals. I think this threw him a bit as he stumbled over his words, but at least I found out he was called Colin. He was too nervous to make conversation, so I dragged him over to watch the dance floor in another attempt to shake Terry. It didn't work.

Colin managed to calm down a bit and we sort of danced at the side of the dance floor for a while. I don't know what had got into the DJ that night, but he really made a hash of the record he was playing then. Every time the song was about to start he went back to the intro. Maybe the record was scratched or someone kept bumping into the DJ's booth. Whatever it was it was certainly breaking the ice with Colin. We were sharing a laugh when Terry slithered back onto the scene.

'I thought you weren't working.' He slimed into my ear, his face well within my personal space.

'I'm not,' I said. 'I told you, Colin is a friend.'

'Does he know about your little sideline?' leered Terry as if it was a threat. 'Do you think he'd still be interested if I told him?' Saying that, he parked himself beside me and gazed out over the dance floor with a smug look on his face. I really wanted to wipe it off for him, but I can't afford to be barred from anywhere. Word soon spreads and you lose your cruising ground, so I just made a dash for the dance floor instead.

Unfortunately, Colin was still unsure of himself and hesitated long enough for Terry to make his move. No matter how energetic I got with my dancing I still couldn't shake him. Eventually it got busy on the dance floor and Terry managed to keep outmanoeuvring me, so my style was severely cramped. I was desperately looking for a way out that didn't involve physical violence when I saw Colin again.

He'd made his way to the dance floor and was dancing alone. The way he kept glancing in my direction let me know he was still interested. The dancing must have been making him hot as he'd loosened his shirt. I could just see a nice thick patch of dark hair peeking through his opened shirt front. I'm a sucker for hairy men and I figured he could be my escape from Terry.

With a deft little side-step I managed to slip around Terry

and position myself so close to Colin that nothing could get in between us. And I mean nothing. Colin was more than willing to accommodate and we put on quite a show. The music took a sultry turn and Colin showed his true colours.

He'd obviously got over whatever had been bothering him before. He reached forward, slipped one arm around my waist and pulled me even closer to him. I synchronised my movements so we seemed to be joined crotch to thigh, gyrating along with the music. He moved his leg slightly so that his firm thigh pressed hard against my stiffening cock. Trapped between our thighs, it swelled to a full erection. He eased back just enough to allow it to slide up my leg to a more comfortable position. Then he carried on rubbing his thigh against it. I could feel the precome starting to ooze out into my jockeys.

I wasn't really ready for that kind of public show so I started to move away. Colin just tightened his grip around my waist and slid his other hand slowly up my back. He pressed gently with it along the sensitive area of my spine until he reached the back of my neck. A jolt of nervous energy flashed through my system as he massaged the middle of my neck with his fingers. Then he took a firm hold and pulled my head toward him. As soon as I was in range he pressed his mouth against mine and started a deep, passionate kiss.

The tempo of the music increased and he thrust his hips faster. The friction against my cock was something else. The feeling was more pronounced for it still being trapped in my underwear. I was really starting to get into this so I hadn't noticed his hand slipping down inside the back of my jeans. At least, not until he had a handful of my firm arse squeezed between his powerful fingers. He tried kneading them like dough so I clenched down hard. I'm proud of my firm arse and I didn't want him thinking it was loose and flabby. He ran his hand over my buns until he found the crack in between.

He stroked the side of his hand along the crack and I felt a mild thrill when he hit the lips of my hole. The bastard must have noticed my jolt against his thigh. He kept circling his finger around the edge of my anus until it loosened. Then he shoved his finger in as far as he could go.

All this time he'd kept his mouth firmly locked around mine. So, when his finger entered deep into my arse and I tried to gasp all I got was a lungful of recycled air. My head started to swim from the force of the kiss. I couldn't focus on the world around us anymore. All I could feel was his thigh rubbing against my swollen cock and his finger massaging the inside of my chute. I was getting close to the heights of orgasm. Then he stopped.

He pulled his finger out of my hole, but kept his hand flat against my arse. He eased the pressure against my back and pulled his head away slightly. It was only then that I opened my eyes and noticed that everyone was staring at us. It must have been closing time; the music had stopped and the lights were back on.

'I think we've given these guys enough of a show, don't you?' he asked.

I just smiled, stunned with embarrassment. I didn't know what had happened to me. Here I was, a hardened pro and he had me feeling at a disadvantage. And I was enjoying it.

'Do you want to come back to my place?'

I just nodded and let him lead the way from the dance floor.

Colin was a lot more reserved in public. He didn't touch me at all for the entire journey in his car, pretending to concentrate on his driving. I suppose it is true that you get a lot of idiots trying to drive after drinking when the clubs shut so you can't be too careful. But he kept his distance when we reached his building as well. He just opened the main door and then ushered me inside. I figured we needed to get to his flat fast before he changed his mind again. As I climbed the stairs two at a time I could feel his eyes burning into my back.

Suddenly, on the second landing, I felt him grab my arse, put his arm around me and pull me back into him. His warm breath tickled my ear as he whispered that this was his flat. Then he pushed his tongue into my earhole and pulled my entire ear into his mouth. A shock of pleasure ran through my entire body as he panted deeply into my ear drum. His tongue ran around the inner edge of my ear, dripping hot saliva as it went, and then thrust back into my hole. My pulse throbbed noisily inside my head and I let myself dissolve into his strong embrace.

Reluctantly, he pulled away, and I leant against the wall while he fumbled with the lock. He managed to get the door open eventually and showed me inside. As he closed the door behind us I engulfed him in a bear hug and pulled him hard against me. I let him experience the full strength of my frame while my powerful hands roamed firmly over his body. I pressed my mouth against his and kissed him deeply. I brought all my experience to play, my hands searching out his pleasure zones, my body crushing his against the wall and my tongue allowing saliva to drool into his mouth.

Suddenly his attitude changed again. He became tense and unresponsive. I let him pull away from me and he ushered me into the lounge. He actually offered me coffee. That was the last thing on my mind, but I figured he might be wanting to play it coy again so I went along with it. His rapid changes of mood were starting to bother me. I could understand cooling down in public, I'd been with enough closet-cases in my time for that. But there was no reason for this sudden frostiness. After all he'd come on to me. And he grabbed me on the stairs. Still, he'd saved me from Terry, so I decided to give him another chance.

I sat on the sofa and waited. He seemed to be taking forever to make the coffee, and I was on the verge of going to look for him when I noticed something very interesting. Most people have magazines lying around on a coffee table for afternoon entertainment or for guests to browse while waiting for coffee. His reading matter was a revelation. A hardback version of *The New Joys of Gay Sex*, the free gay papers and a couple of hard-core porn magazines. He obviously wasn't a prude, despite recent impressions.

I started to thumb through the magazines. Hey, I needed to do something to keep on the boil. And this magazine was certainly hot. It was from my favourite company. They specialise in pictures of really masculine men. You know the sort; rugged looks, heavy muscles, hairy bodies and huge cocks. Well this magazine was based on one of their videos. It had pictures featuring two of their hottest studs. I'd always had a weakness for these two, but hadn't managed to get a copy of the video.

The plot, such as it was, revolved around a rugged rancher who wanted some help around his place and a heavily muscled guy who applied for the job. Obviously it didn't take them long to get down to the job and he proved his credentials straight away. There didn't seem to be much work going on though, they were too busy fucking everywhere; in a barn, on a tractor, in a field, in a bunkhouse, on a hilltop. Just seeing all that tanned, glistening, sweaty muscle captured in action was making me wish I was in the pictures with them instead of waiting here for Colin and his coffee. I figured I had been fucked around enough so I stripped off and really got into the mood. I closed my eyes and imagined myself on the ranch with the guys in the magazine.

There I was, first day on the job delivering mail, and I had a special delivery for this ranch. I couldn't leave it in the mailbox because it had to be signed for. I called out as I got near the house, but there was no reply. I looked around for a while and thought I heard noises coming from the barn. The door was open so I just walked in. There they were. Stark bollock naked. Two muscular giants. Sweat running over their hard bodies as they wrestled in the straw. Their huge arms bulged with solid muscle, dark veins showing through their deep tans. They were growling at each other and grunting with the effort of trying to get control. They seemed pretty evenly matched. Not an ounce of fat on either of them. As they twisted and turned I caught glimpses of their cocks and they were pretty well-matched there too. One was slightly longer, but the other was thicker. Both were totally hard and oozing precome as they slapped against firm, ridged stomachs.

One guy stumbled and lost his footing in the straw. The other took his chance and grabbed him by the cock to keep him off balance. He forced him down over a bale and dropped his whole weight on top of him. I could hear the air rushing out of the first guy's lungs as he was crushed against the rough straw. The other pressed his advantage, grabbed a powerful arm and thrust it hard up behind the muscular back. I was nearly deafened by the deep yell of pain and frustration. The trapped guy tried to struggle, but the other had the leverage he needed to keep him down where he wanted him. Eventually he went limp, resigned to his fate. The other guy eased the pressure on his arm, but obviously didn't trust him fully as he kept a firm grip and the tension was obvious in his huge muscles just waiting to spring back into action. The first guy got to his feet and that's when I got my first good look at it. His massive physique was spectacular, but even that didn't hide the enormous size of his cock. It stretched straight up past his navel and was easily as thick as my wrist. Clear juice dribbled from the giant head and ran along a thick vein toward his heavy, hairy ballsac.

I must have made a noise in my surprise, because they suddenly stopped and turned toward me. My mouth went dry and I couldn't speak. They glanced at each other and then charged in my direction. Part of me wanted to run, but I couldn't tear myself away from the sight of all that muscle heading toward me. Before I could recover I was grabbed by four huge arms and carried over to the bales of straw. I felt the powerful hands tear my clothes from me until I was totally naked. The straw scratched at my bare skin when they threw me down onto it. One man grabbed my wrists, the other my ankles and they lifted me high into the air. The guy at my head pushed his great cock over my lips, past my teeth, along my tongue and deep into my throat. I began to gag against the thickness, but had other things to worry about. My legs were pulled as far apart as they would go and I could feel the tip of the head of the other guy's truly enormous cock pushing against the tight ring of my arse. There was no way I could hold out against all the muscle that was behind that battering ram, and it started to force its way home. I could feel my hole tearing as it struggled to let the vast tube pass through. My guts were being crushed on the inside and it was absolutely pulverising my joy-spot. Then I heard the creak.

I opened my eyes and Colin stood in the doorway. By this time I was so hot I would have shagged anything that couldn't move fast enough to escape. I slid off the sofa and prowled toward him. My whole body was aching for sex. I hadn't been this turned-on for a long time. I grabbed him and crushed his body against mine, kissing him deeply and ravishing him with my hands. I didn't care that he wasn't responding. In fact I hadn't noticed until he pushed me away.

I could feel the blood pounding in my temples as he tried to make some sort of excuse. The words didn't mean much to me as I was struggling to keep control. My body was shaking as I forced myself back into my clothes before I did something he was going to regret. He grabbed my arm to stop me, but I pulled it away, just stopping myself from hitting him. The jerk actually gave me his business card and asked me to call him. I crushed it in my frustration and shoved past him, getting away from there as fast as I could.

When I got outside I stopped and tried to regain control. A few deep breaths calmed me down a bit, but my fists were still clenched when I pushed them into my pockets out of the cold. I was still too wound up to go home so I decided to walk round to my usual cruising ground. It wasn't too late. I might get some action and save the night from being a total waste after all.

Chapter Two

COLIN

I watched his firm, round buttocks swaying inside the tight, faded jeans as he used his powerful legs to climb the stairs two at a time. I brought him to a halt on the landing by reaching forward to cup his anus in the palm of my hand and press my fingers firmly against the spot just behind his balls. The response was a mixture between a squeal of surprise and a gasp of pleasure. I put my other arm around his waist, pulling him back into me and spoke gently into his ear.

'This is the place,' I breathed as I indicated the door to my flat, then shoved my tongue into his earhole and sucked the rest of his ear into my mouth. I felt his whole body go rigid and he reached back, grasping my buttocks to pull us even closer. I ground my painfully hard cock against his arse. I gave his ear a serious tongue-lashing and hugged him tight, losing myself in the pleasure of his response and the heat of the passion between us.

Eventually I pulled away and he leaned against the wall by the door as I fumbled for my keys. Although I was convinced I'd locked up before I left, the key wouldn't turn as I expected it to. I chalked it up to another lapse of concentration due to rushing to get out, opened the other lock (a Yale this time) and pushed the door open.

I closed the door behind us and turned to be greeted with a passionate embrace. Our mouths clamped together and our tongues jostled to explore them as our hands roved over the outsides of our bodies. I felt the erogenous zones of my taste buds react as his saliva drooled along his tongue onto mine.

Then I noticed it. The soft glow creeping out beneath the bedroom door. Feeling the change in my mood, he pulled away and looked at me enquiringly. I tried to make light of it, guiding him into the lounge and asking him to wait while I put the kettle on. All the same I couldn't shake the feeling of foreboding which replaced the lust in the pit of my stomach.

While the kettle boiled I walked to the bedroom and eased the door open. There he was. Tim, sprawled across the bed fast asleep.

I closed the door quietly and my brain raced to keep up with my emotions as I made the journey back to the lounge. First I cursed Tim for coming back. Then I cursed myself for not changing the locks or getting my keys back. When I walked into the lounge my thoughts became even more jumbled. My companion for the night had made use of his time waiting alone to remove his clothes and now lay on the couch gently stroking his erect cock.

For some time I merely stood and watched as he remained lost in the privacy of masturbation shared only with whatever image reigned behind the closed lids of his eyes. It was a particularly arousing sight. He looked even better out of his clothes, fulfilling the promises made by the tight-fitting material. His left hand held the back of his head, showing the full effect of the athletic bulge of his bicep and the taut sinews of his forearm. His right leg hung over the side of the couch, bent slightly at the knee with only the heel of his foot on the floor, displaying the kind of thigh and calf definition of a regular runner or cyclist. His cock suited his body perfectly. It was long and slender yet powerful. As cliched as it sounds the overall effect truly resembled a jungle cat in human form, seemingly at ease, but with all the magnificent muscles bunched below the surface, poised ready to strike when necessary. His cock was obviously ready to strike as it leaked pre-come which he spread liberally along the shaft causing it to glisten with lubrication.

I moved forward into the room and a creaking floorboard betrayed my presence. He opened his eyes lazily, turned his head in my direction and smiled. As he slid off the couch and prowled toward me he looked even more like a predator moving in for the kill. 'I was getting tired of waiting,' he said, pulling me to him and kissing me hard. My whole body ached with lust, but my mind kept wandering to Tim in the bedroom, wondering what trouble had brought him back this time. As I felt a hand undo the fly of my jeans and slip inside, I finally surrendered to my apprehension. 'I'm sorry,' I said, gently easing him away from me.

'What?' he snapped, clearly annoyed at being interrupted.

'Look, I'm really sorry, but something personal has cropped up and I'm afraid I've got to deal with that now. Please don't take it as a rejection.'

As I spoke he had gone to his clothes, shaking with anger, and began to pull them on. 'What's happened? No, don't tell me, let me guess. You had a blazing row with your lover earlier this evening and stormed out in a fit of pique. You came on to me in the club, feeling sorry for yourself and angry at him, and brought me back to spite him. Now I've either served my purpose or you've got cold feet.'

By now he was fully clothed and stood facing me. Trying to defuse the situation, I placed a pacifying hand on his arm, which he jerked away. 'It's not like that at all. I just can't explain right now. Please accept that it's nothing personal. Give me a call another time.' I took one of my cards out of my pocket and offered it to him. He took it, bemused, and then crushed it in his fist before shoving past me and storming out to the front door.

'You wouldn't like what I'd call you if I did,' he snarled as he left.

I spent a few minutes in the kitchen trying to settle down while the kettle boiled again and I prepared coffee for Tim and tea for myself. Unfortunately I didn't succeed in feeling any calmer; instead I brooded on the situation and my anger rose to fill the gap left by my earlier passion and replacing the lesser frustration I had felt.

When Tim walked out on me I, like so many other lovers before me, felt as if my life was over. I felt that I had put so much work into the relationship that I was being cheated when he left it so effortlessly. To make matters worse, he only walked out of the relationship, not out of my life. I still saw him out on the scene with his new lover. I made sure they didn't see me. They seemed so happy together and all I did was allow myself to be eaten up by the feeling that I should have what they shared.

Oh, it took a while, but I finally accepted what my friends had been telling me all along. I realised that I was living my life like the lyrics of songs from the Seventies. The pain eased and I began the slow process of rebuilding. It helped that Tim and his lover had disappeared from the scene. I didn't care why. I was just pleased I was recovering. The less I saw of him, the less I hurt. Eventually I felt so secure that I could contact Tim again and try to salvage whatever chance of friendship might remain. It started with cards on his birthday and Christmas and progressed to regular letters. I didn't get a reply, but he never was much of a writer.

I didn't have another relationship after Tim. I hadn't had one before him either. I threw myself into a long line of one-night stands: I was making up for lost time. I didn't intend them all to be casual sexual encounters, but none of them was as fulfilling as the time I spent with Tim. There was always something missing. It's amazing how you can get so used to someone in such a short period of time. Tim and I were together for less than a year.

And now he'd just turned up again and ruined my latest chance of a romantic evening. Just like every other time. Before the great split Tim had 'left' me several times. It almost became a routine. I would say or do something to upset him and we would argue. Then would come the ceremonial returning of the keys and he would rage out of the flat ordering me not to contact him. He always came back within the week. Somehow or other he'd missed me and wanted to try again. For my part I'd cried myself to sleep each night he was away as I hugged the pillow tightly where he should be. There were even nights when I couldn't face going to bed but slept on the couch instead. Eventually I'd force myself to face up to the world beyond my front door and I'd meet someone while I was out there. When I started to get close to them Tim would come back and everything would get mixed up again. That's why it took so long to recover when he finally walked out for good. I kept expecting him to come back. Even though he left me for someone else that time. After all, he'd kept his set of keys to the flat for a change.

It was time to face him. I opened the bedroom door and looked down at his sprawling form. When he left he'd sworn he was going to 'get a body' if it killed him. He was going to get to the gym at least six days a week and get a decent tan if it cost him his last penny on sunbed sessions. From the sight on the bed he'd been true to his word.

What had been a lithe, youthful figure was now a mound of bronzed developing muscle. His arms bulged as he cradled his head in them. His shoulders were broad and rippled as they rose and fell with each deep breath. His torso tapered down towards the solid, dimpled cheeks of his arse. His thighs looked massive and inviting as they lay spread wide across the bed and his calves pointed up to the ceiling even in this relaxed state. His sleep had obviously been troubled as the bedclothes showed signs of restlessness. As I watched I felt my mood mellow as my heart-strings were tugged. The tugging was repeated in my groin. Just looking at him had always been enough to give me an erection. Shit, even thinking about sex with him was often enough.

I put the mugs down on a bedside cabinet and sat beside him on the bed. I took a deep breath to steady myself, placed a hand on his nearest shoulder and shook it. The head of tousled hair raised from the pillow and turned in my direction as the deep hazel eyes struggled to focus.

'Okay, what happened this time?' I snapped.

He looked up into my eyes and I started to melt. With one swift motion he twisted his body until his head was in my lap and threw his powerful arms around my waist. That did it. I was now totally mush. I had always adored his childlike innocence and naivete which he showed unabashed with gestures like this. I stroked his hair reassuringly as he spoke.

He told how his time with Pete had been so awful. How they were so different, with no shared interests. How Pete had so many friends he had little time for just the two of them. How Pete had seemed cold and aloof against Tim's advances, which must have really hurt as I knew the affection that Tim was capable of giving. They'd hardly had sex in all the time they'd been seeing each other. In the end he'd decided that

Pete just didn't love him enough and that he needed to get out before he lost the remains of his self respect. This was the only place he could think of to run to.

Flattered that he still thought of me with such fondness, I slipped my arms around his shoulders and hugged him tight. Despite myself, the feeling of his hard body against mine after all this time brought my cock to life. As it bulged forward I felt his hot breath against it and realised I had left my flies undone after my earlier encounter.

'Well, I can tell you're pleased to see me,' he said as he looked up at me again. This time his eyes contained a wicked sparkle. 'Some things never change.' He wiped the pre-come from my cock-slit with his hand and engulfed my knob with his mouth. I groaned from the very base of my being and arched my body back against the headboard in ecstasy as he buried his face in my jeans. He ran his tongue expertly around the head of my cock in between sliding his mouth up and down the shaft for what felt like forever. I put my hands against the back of his head and pressed down as I felt the urgent pressure building from my balls. Suddenly he pulled his head away.

'Get your clothes off,' he commanded and I complied.

I felt him watching as I undressed with my back to him, but when I turned around he was bent over removing his underwear, which was all he ever slept in. The sight was so appealing I didn't stand a chance of resisting. I buried my face in his arse and he fell forward onto the bed. I ran my tongue around the inside of the cheeks of his arse and nibbled them lightly before sucking on them. I moved my head to a more central position and lapped around the edge of his anus. I recognised the still familiar groan of ecstasy as I slid down the flesh between his anus and his balls. I sucked gently on the area that seems to be an extension of the cock behind the ball sac and pressed hard with my tongue. I felt the saliva flow onto his skin and knew I was ready to move on.

I gently caught the edge of his anus between my lips and pressed my chin against his balls. I caressed his entire hole with the flat of my tongue and saw a slight shiver force its way along his spine. I pulled back for a moment, separated his cheeks with my hands, looked down at the glistening pink rosette and took a deep breath before diving in.

I pushed my tongue as far into his anus as I could and moved it around occasionally, curling it as I did so. I felt his body go rigid as I entered him and appreciated for the first time the extent of his new strength as his powerful buttocks clamped against my face.

I was beginning to run out of air when he suddenly relaxed and his breathing became regular as it always had when he was really getting into the effects of a good rimming. Panting, I raised my head and stroked his loosened anus with the tip of a finger. He raised his hips slightly and pressed back into my hand. I reached around with my other hand and grasped his cock firmly. As I stroked it I noticed how well it matched his new body. Its impressive length was by far overshadowed by the fact it was so wide and solid.

He grunted as my finger got too adventurous and I noted that he hadn't changed his mind about experimenting with being fucked. He never was into that. At least, assuming it hadn't only been me he'd denied entry to his arsehole. I took my hand away and tried to push my face back in its place, but he had other ideas. He pulled my hand from his cock and climbed off the bed.

He turned toward me and pulled me against him in a crushing embrace. His mouth locked against mine as he pushed his tongue inside and flicked it around against my teeth. His strong arms squeezed the breath from my body and his mouth sucked it into his. I started to feel light-headed. I felt his iron-hard cock against mine as he ground our hips together. The pressure against my ribcage eased and he slid his hands down my back. A shock passed through my body as he shoved his fingers hard against the crack of my arse then lifted me effortlessly and threw me onto the bed.

The weight of his muscular torso pressed me into the mattress as he swallowed my cock again. I closed my eyes and savoured the pleasure I felt, allowing my hands to roam freely exploring the bulging muscles of his powerful body. I felt a rush of cold air against my tender cock as he pulled his head back. Then the tantalising dampness of saliva falling onto the slit of my knob and trickling over the head and down the length of my cock to form a pool at its base and around my balls. When he decided it was lubricated enough he clamped it in the vice-like grip of a strong hand and pumped it savagely.

I writhed and twisted in delight beneath his firm body, trying to change my position to reciprocate. Eventually I found my head and shoulders were hanging over the side of the bed. I opened my eyes and saw his heavy balls above me. I wrapped an arm around each of his massive thighs and lifted my head until I could reach the base of his scrotum with my tongue. As I licked and sucked at the tender flesh I pulled on his legs to support my balance. To keep his, he released his grip on my cock and pressed heavily into the bed with his hands.

I sucked each of his balls in turn into my mouth, pulling on them and pressing them against the roof of my mouth with my tongue. He yelped and pulled away, so I changed my attention to a less tender area. I leant my head back and stretched my neck until I caught his knob in my mouth. I strained to slide my lips up his cock, feeling my jaw pull as it struggled with the thickness of his shaft. I heard him groan as his knob stopped against the back of my throat. With some effort I relaxed and swallowed hard. His thighs clamped against the sides of my head and we stayed like that for some time, with me swallowing and massaging his cockhead with my throat while my tongue struggled to stroke as far around his shaft as it could.

Eventually I felt him shift his weight onto his hands and begin to pump his hips slowly. I opened my mouth and throat as wide as I could to give way to his persistent thrusts as he slowly and expertly fucked my face.

He stopped, still lodged deep inside me, and shifted his position again, grabbing my legs and pulling them apart. I felt him drool again onto the base of my balls. Then a second gob hit dead centre on my arsehole. A strong finger pushed the spit inside and I gasped, swallowing his cock even further. The finger thrust into my arse several times and then pulled out, only to be joined by a second. I groaned with pleasure as the fingers twisted and turned, stretching the edges of my anus and making my hole beg for more. He pulled his fingers out of my arse and his cock out of my throat, leaving both feeling empty and desperate. Then he pushed both back in forcefully and as far as he could before fucking both ends of me in unison.

I gasped for breath, gagging on his huge cock, coating it with saliva and revelling in the pleasure in my arse as it created its own lubrication. Then he pulled his cock out of my mouth, dripping saliva onto my face, and climbed onto the bed. Positioning himself between my legs he was able to push a third finger into my arse. Then a fourth and his thumb. He pressed them deep and spread them apart to loosen the hole. He pulled them out, grabbed a leg in each of his hands and pushed them over my head. I felt the enormous head of his cock press against my anus and looked up through my legs at his beautiful body. His face was a study of concentration as his cock failed to gain entry. I caught hold of my ankles and freed his hands to guide it in. I cried out in agony as the huge cock pushed smoothly and relentlessly into my hole. It didn't stop until it pressed hard against my prostate.

I looked up at him again and this time his eyes were closed as he savoured the moment. Then he looked down at me and smiled wickedly. He put his hands on my thighs and shifted his weight onto them and began to find his rhythm. A mixture of gasps and grunts and yells escaped from me as I felt the combination of his wide cock stretching my arse as far as it would go and the hard knob ramming home against my prostate.

My cries grew louder as I felt my love muscle contract and my balls fill up. My whole body tensed and my cock and prostate jerked in the most powerful orgasm I could remember. I'd definitely remember this one as it wasn't accompanied by an ejaculation, but was my first truly deep and dry orgasm.

Tim looked down at my flushed face and smiled again as the muscles in my arse started to relax once more. He began to pump his still hard cock slowly. I begged him to pull out, but he refused, thrusting deeper with each stroke. My hopes were raised as he pulled the head of his cock back as far as my sphincter, only to plunge me back into agony as he thrust his full length back into me. This seemed to go on forever until I felt his hand grab hold of my cock again and pump it forcefully. I looked up at him and admired his gym-trained body. Sweat glistened on his deep tan and ran down his broad chest. His biceps bulged as his arm moved his hand along my cock. My cock which suddenly demanded all my attention as it seemed to swell to bursting point. My eyes closed and my breath stopped as I bordered on ejaculation.

Then I roared out the breath I had been holding and my head snapped up from the bed as every muscle in my body clenched to force the sperm to fly out of my cock and high into the air. As my head dashed back and forth I noticed Tim's abdominals bunch and his face flush and I felt his cock thrust as deeply as it could against my clenched muscles before pumping a massive load into my arse.

Totally spent, I collapsed back on the bed. Tim's cock slid easily out of my arse and he fell forward onto me. I gazed deeply into his eyes and said, 'I love you.' He laid his head on my chest and we fell into a deep exhausted sleep.

I awoke next morning sore and aching but content. Then I realised I was alone in the bed. I staggered to the bathroom and left the bath running as I looked for Tim. I expected to find him sat in front of the TV with his breakfast like in the old days, but there was no sign of him anywhere. I went to the kitchen and prepared a hot drink, still clutching the hope that he'd only gone to run an errand. Then I noticed it.

I was vaguely aware of the bath overflowing in the distance as I realised, 'At least this time the bastard's left his keys.'

Chapter Three

TIM

It was one more bad night in a long series of bad nights. And it was supposed to be special. It was all starting to get to me. I emptied the last dregs of wine from the bottle. I raised my glass to the rapidly diminishing candle in a toast to 'absent friends'. Then I drained the glass in one swift sharp movement. With a deep sigh I stood, extinguished the candle and cleared the table.

In the kitchen I separated the unused cutlery and put it away before putting my place setting into a bowl. I turned the oven off, took out the plate and emptied the dried-up contents into the pedal-bin. I put the grimy plate into the bowl and ran some water in to let the crockery soak. The washing-up could wait until morning. With one more glance around the room I turned off the light.

In the bathroom I followed my usual nightly routine. After replacing the used mouthwash and toothpaste in the bathroom cabinet I looked at my reflection in the mirrored door. Could I still fend off the competition? What more could I do? I already went to the gym six days a week. I'd got the stretch marks to prove it. I used all the right potions and lotions, but still the signs of age were beginning to show. My hair is thinning and my looks are fading. The 'laughter-lines' are turning to wrinkles and my tanned skin is looking more like tanned hide. With another sigh I turned off the light and went to bed.

I undressed in the bedroom, carefully folding my clothes and placing them in the closet. Dirty laundry goes in the hamper in the corner of the room. I climbed into the large bed, pulled the covers tightly around myself, hugged the pillow to my chest and went to sleep.

I awoke with the bed undulating gently beneath me. I opened my eyes, but did not speak. I didn't trust myself to avoid another argument.

'I didn't mean to disturb you.'

'It's a water bed, it's hard to get into without causing a disturbance.'

'I'm sorry.'

'For what?'

'For everything.'

'That's mighty big of you. Although I'm sure there are several major floods, wars, famines and other natural disasters for which you are not directly responsible.'

'I'm sorry I was late. I'm sorry I did not let you know in advance. I'm sorry dinner was spoiled. I'm sorry I missed our anniversary.'

'So am I.'

'What?'

'Well, it's not exactly the first time you've let me down is it? In fact you're rather making a habit of it.'

'Oh, not that again. Perhaps I should not have come back at all.'

'No, I didn't mean . . .' I thought back to all the ruined meals, all the wasted evenings waiting for a phone call, all the wasted energy spent trying to explain the problem in the past,

'No . . . perhaps you're right; you shouldn't have.'

I got out of bed, walked to the spare bedroom, quietly closed the door, climbed into the small single bed, pulled the sheets tightly around myself, clutched the pillows to my chest and cried myself to sleep.

Once again my sleep was disturbed by Pete. This time he had managed to climb into bed without waking me and wrapped himself around me. Not content with violating every bit of my personal space he was also mauling me in an attempt at personal gratification. I suppose it could have been his idea of trying to make amends, but it was totally the wrong thing to do at that time. I hate being roused from a deep slumber at the best of times. And my emotions were already running high. He had just added personal violation to his long list of crimes for the evening.

'That's your answer to everything isn't it,' I yelled as I pushed his hand from my chest where it had been toying with my nipple. He knows that every erogenous zone in my body is linked to those studs. And he was abusing that knowledge. I threw the covers back and jumped from the bed. He just lay there in stunned silence as all my frustrations poured out over him. 'Sex. Tim's feeling touchy so it must be his hormones. A good steamy session will sort him out.' At this point I turned and stormed over to the wardrobe. All the time lashing out at my insensitive lover. 'But, no, I'm not being fair. You wouldn't have thought that.' I slammed the wardrobe door open and began to root through the spare clothes we kept in there. 'That would have meant considering my feelings even a little.' I began to struggle into a pair of jogging pants. 'And you just aren't capable of that.' On went a sweatshirt, momentarily muffling my verbal tirade. 'You only ever think of yourself, you selfish shit. You were probably feeling frustrated because you hadn't had your nookie ration for the night and thought you'd help yourself.' I reached behind me to grab a jacket and returned to the bed. Looming over his prone form I reached my climax. 'Well, as far as I'm concerned you can just do everything for yourself from now on.' I straightened up, jerked the bedroom door open and made the best exit of my life. In the hall I paused only long enough to slip on a pair of trainers before rushing out of the front door. I couldn't stop to think or I might change my mind.

After wandering aimlessly for some time (I hadn't picked up a watch before I left) I began to cool down a little. I hadn't forgiven Pete. I was just feeling less emotional and able to think more rationally. I didn't want to go home. He would see that as capitulation on my part. Where else could I go? I hadn't picked up any money or credit cards either so finding a room for the night was out of the question. I had no close friends of my own to impose upon. I give my all to a relationship so we only had joint friends. And I just knew they would side with him. They always had before if the subject of his insensitivity was touched on. 'He doesn't mean anything by it. He's just been working so hard lately. You're overreacting again.' I couldn't face that.

Nor could I face another night sleeping rough. Once was more than enough. It was years before when I was too young to know better. I'd gone out for the night with a group of friends and somehow we got separated. I never found out what happened, but I lost my lift home and didn't have enough money on me for the taxi fare. I tried the buses and trains, but they didn't run that late. I spent the night on a bench at the train station. It was an open plan station with little shelter and I was amazed I didn't get hypothermia. Just the memory of that night was enough to chill me to the bone.

With a little shiver I slipped into the jacket I had grabbed as an afterthought. It didn't quite fit as I hadn't worn it for years and I'd gained a fair bit of size across my shoulders. I smiled at the thought that all the visits to the gym were paying off. Then something hard in one of the pockets rattled against my hips. Curious, I felt inside and encountered a set of keys. Colin's keys. God, it had been a while. Would he mind my turning up out of the blue? Did I have a choice? I decided not, got my bearings and started the walk over to his place.

I stood outside the entrance to Colin's flats and hesitated. It had been a long time since I'd seen him. And I had treated him rather badly in the past. Perhaps if I'd replied to some of the Christmas and birthday cards? I reviewed my other options. None. I was sure Colin would understand. That's the kind of guy he was. Solid, dependable and, I suppose, a bit of a pushover. I pressed his bell. No response. I pressed it again. Still nothing. Perhaps he was asleep? Perhaps he was out? I fumbled with the keys in my pocket. Could I just let myself in? No. That wouldn't be fair. But I had walked forever to get there. And I needed to use the toilet. I never could just go in the street like most other guys I knew. And why should I when I had access to a perfectly good bathroom right here. I was sure Colin would understand. I opened the door and went in out of the cold.

I paused again outside his door. I knocked loudly in case he'd somehow not heard the bell. Still no response. I tried the door. It was locked. He was out, then. I had just unlocked the mortice and put the key in the Yale when a thought struck me. What if he'd moved? I could be calmly entering the home of a total stranger. But no, Colin would have let me know if he'd moved. Even though I hadn't been in contact with him for absolutely ages, he always went out of his way to let me know where he was at any given time in case I felt the need to. And besides, my bladder was in danger of emptying right where I stood. If he had moved I'd just nip in, use the bathroom and leave again. There'd be no harm done and no-one would be any the wiser. I opened the door and stepped inside.

Once over the threshold I headed straight for the bathroom. What a relief that was. As my cramped bladder began to return to normal I looked around. I also began to worry. The bathroom had been decorated. I knew it had been a while, but it wasn't like Colin to be so industrious. All the time I knew him his flat had been just the wrong side of being untidy enough to look lived in. If you were honest, it was a dump. The flat itself was nice enough, so was Colin, he just couldn't be bothered with housework. He was also the world's worst hoarder, so every surface in the place was covered by clutter which he used as an excuse not to clean under it.

The new decor was certainly to Colin's taste. The wallpaper was beige and shiny, the new fittings were mahogany stained, the walls held portraits of scantily clad muscular young men and there was an abundance of those floating candles on metal stands that he liked so much. I wondered if he'd got a professional decorator in until I noticed the sure signs of an impatient amateur: the misshapen cut around the toilet waste-pipes, slight bulges on corners that hadn't quite been brushed down properly, little patches of paper pasted over gaps where it had been cut too short and the curtains tied back with bits of string. Having recognised Colin's trademark laziness, I wondered what had brought on the unusual bout of effort needed to see the task through. In my day he would have stopped as soon as things got awkward, leaving several bare walls and a paste table with half a bucket of paste congealing in another room. Perhaps he'd found himself another lover? Once again I wondered if I might be intruding.

As I left the bathroom I decided he would have told me if

he had met someone else. And, besides, now that my emotion-charged adrenaline high had died down and my bladder was empty, I was feeling pretty exhausted. Colin would understand if I crashed in his spare bed.

Unfortunately Colin's new industrious streak hadn't lasted as far as the spare bedroom. The sofa-bed was covered in junk, including the old bathroom fixtures, and drying laundry fought for space with scattered decorating tools. I didn't have the energy to sort that lot out. I went into Colin's room, stripped off and climbed into his bed. If Colin came back while I was there I'd explain what had happened. He'd understand.

I was shaken awake from one of those dreams you don't remember in detail, but remain disturbed by it. I just wasn't destined for a good night's rest. I was about to give Pete a piece of my mind when I saw Colin, remembered where I was and why I was there. Colin was sitting on the edge of the bed and leaning over me. I looked up and saw nothing but concern in his big brown eyes. He never did try to hide his feelings.

That was a major problem in a relationship with Colin; his emotions poured out of those beautiful, big brown eyes. You could drown in the ocean of emotion he produced. And he felt everything so deeply. Try telling him you couldn't make it to the pictures because you had to work overtime; try telling him you'd just broken the old towel rail in the bathroom, try telling him you didn't want him to go into debt buying you those expensive gifts; try telling him things aren't working out and you should spend some time apart. Try telling a toddler their favourite puppy's just been squashed by a juggernaut. Same effect. Oh, he didn't make a scene. He made a big show of being calm and understanding. But you knew. You could see the emotions fighting to break out in those eyes.

This time those eyes weren't acting as a floodgate for his

emotions so much as a sponge for mine. I couldn't face him, so I threw my head into his lap and poured out all my troubles. I don't remember the specifics, but I know I bared my soul to him. Maybe I just needed someone to listen to me for a change and I thought he'd understand. He'd always made such a show of being caring and considerate in the past. All this emotion was so painful I'm sure I had my eyes closed to fight back the tears. As I slowed to a halt, whether I'd run out of words or breath I don't know, I opened my eyes and that's when I saw it.

His flies were undone and he had a raging erection poking toward my face. Even worse, he put his arms around my shoulders and pushed me toward it.

I realised my mistake. Colin was no better than the others. When it came down to it he'd do or say anything to get into your pants. I'd forgotten his overactive libido. I looked at him with as much disgust as I could manage, wiped the slime from the top of his cock and shoved it in my mouth. I tried to show him what a blow-job was like without emotion. I hoped he'd realise the error of his ways, but it didn't work. Perhaps he'd been too long without sex so anything was welcome. He was definitely getting off on this. I think he noticed that I was trying to rush things because he put his hands on my head to control my movements.

I decided I'd had enough. If he wanted sex that badly I was going to give it to him. I was going to get rid of all my hurt and anger at men in general by raping this specific one. I pulled my head from his groin and told him to strip.

In hindsight turning my back on him to remove my underwear was a mistake. He must have broken every record to get out of his clothes. I was still tugging my briefs from around my ankles when he shoved me onto the bed and pushed his face into my arse. Why is it you can never fart when you really want to?

I've never been into rimming. It always seemed so distasteful. I could never get my mind past the thought of the normal use for that orifice. There was no way I'd put my face near someone else's dumpchute. And there was definitely not a chance in Hell of my kissing someone who'd been delving in mine.

Mind you, it feels really good when it's done properly. And Colin sure knew how to do it. As he nibbled and sucked around the cheeks of my arse I began to forget how repulsive I thought the act was. When his tongue found the pleasure spot between my arsehole and balls I even forgot how upset I was with him. He sucked my tender flesh into his mouth and massaged it with his firm but pliant tongue. His hot breath brought goose-bumps to the surface as it rolled over my moist skin.

He moved his mouth to my arsehole and I shivered as he stroked it with the entire length of his tongue. I felt him pull my cheeks apart, probably in preparation for shoving his face further in. My sensitivities returned to the fore and I tried to clamp my arse shut against him. It was too late. He already had his face between my buttocks and his tongue shoved deep into my hole. I couldn't fight it any more. The tension flowed out of my entire body and I gave in to the soporific tendencies I always had when Colin expertly used his mouth for my sexual gratification. As usual, I was totally gone. No amount of narcotics could move me to this plane of reality. I'd forgotten everything that was wrong with the world. Hell, I'd even forgotten the world existed at that point. That was when he brought me back with a jolt.

The little bastard wasn't satisfied with the great sex we were having. He had to try it on. He knew I wasn't into anything solid up my arse and yet he thought I wouldn't notice when he shoved his finger in. The selfish git wasn't getting away with that. It was time I took control again.

I climbed off the bed, pulled him to me and squeezed for all

I was worth. It would have been so easy to continue the pressure of the bearhug until his ribs cracked. Unfortunately, he seemed to be getting off on this domination kick as much as I was. He pushed his face against mine and kissed me deeply. No, he was enjoying that too much. I had the upper hand here. I was the more powerful. I was the injured party. And now I was going to take advantage of him.

I released my hold long enough to get hold of his arse and toss him onto the bed. As forcefully as I could I wrapped my mouth around his cock and sucked. I was tempted to sink my teeth into the tender flesh, but decided that would be too easy. Besides he was so hard by now I'd probably chip a tooth. I pulled my head back and let saliva drip from my tongue onto his knob. Then I got a firm grip on his cock and yanked on it as hard and as fast as I could manage. The plan was to jerk him off as quickly as I could so he'd still be left feeling unsatisfied, but he was enjoying even that too much. I knew I was in control, he just hadn't got the idea through his thick skull yet.

It was like trying to keep hold of a wet fish. He writhed and squirmed about until he somehow managed to get his head between my legs and shoved his tongue into my balls. He'd caught me totally by surprise and I was so off balance that I fell onto the bed when he pulled against my thighs. By the time I regained my balance he had my cock in his mouth and was going to town on one of his famous blow-jobs. I knew that I'd lose it if I let him carry on. He had a natural talent as a cock-sucker which had always sent me shooting straight to heavenly ecstasy where my entire body turned to mush while he worked away sucking and licking and swallowing for an eternity.

I was determined to keep control of this situation. I was supposed to be dominating him. Mind you, the feeling of his hot mouth stretched around my hard cock was fantastic. I decided I could make my point by fucking his face. I balanced my weight on my hands and began to pump my hips slowly. At first he resisted, trying to keep the pace by rocking his head and sucking and swallowing, but he soon found out I was too big for him to fight. I pulled my cock out until the very tip was against his lips and then slowly thrust back in until the head hammered against the back of his throat. He always did have trouble taking my size without bruising his tonsils. That suited me fine this time. It would serve him right if he had a croaky voice for a few days. I continued to pump with my hips, letting my cock slide almost out of his mouth each time and then thrusting back as far and as deep as I could.

I don't know if he'd been practising, but suddenly he managed to relax the muscles of his throat so that I slid in right to the root of my cock. I felt his lips stretched wide against the base of my member and his nose buried into my pubic hair. This wasn't hurting him enough. I decided to take my domination a step further.

Leaving him gagged by my thick dick, I shifted my weight to my hips until they forced his head against the side of the mattress. He was now trapped beneath my bodyweight. I pulled his legs apart and started to go to work on his other end. I spat once on his arsehole and shoved my index finger inside in one swift movement. He certainly felt that. He swallowed my cock even deeper. I thrust my finger in and out a few times until he got comfortable with that. I felt his deep moans rumble against my cock, still lodged in his throat. I slipped a second finger into his tight hole. For a few moments I just twisted my fingers around and pushed them apart, stretching the edges of his arse and rubbing against the inside wall. Then I started to finger-fuck his arse while matching the rhythm with my cock fucking his face.

He was really getting off on this. I felt him loosen up at

both ends as he gave himself over to me completely. The trouble was that it's not a very comfortable position. There I was trying to balance on one hand on the bed and keep a rhythm going between the other hand and my hips. It was starting to feel like hard work. And I was supposed to be punishing him. I pulled my cock out of his mouth and climbed onto the bed, ready to move to the next stage. I'd never really tried fisting before.

Shifting my position slightly, I managed to slide a third finger into his arse. It was a bit of a struggle when I tried a fourth and my thumb. He reached his limit with my third knuckle. I wasn't in the mood to get some proper lubrication or wait for him to relax and stretch so I gave up on the idea of a complete fisting. I gave him one last stretch for good measure and decided to fuck him senseless.

Hauling his legs into the air I positioned my cock against his hole. Unfortunately my aim wasn't very good from this angle and I had some trouble getting it in. Colin obviously didn't know what I had planned because he decided to help out. He grabbed his ankles so I could use my hands to get my cock into position. Was he going to get a surprise! Once I'd got the angle right I rammed my ample cock as far as it would go into his arse. Sure I'd stretched it a bit, but I was still intent on playing rough. He cried out in pain and looked up at me with a wide-eyed expression. I just smiled, put my hands on his thighs for balance and got into the rhythm of a long hard fuck. Slowly pulling out as far as I could and then quickly ramming back in until my balls hit his arse.

I'd forgotten just how noisy Colin is while getting fucked. He grunted, he growled, he cried out and he shouted while I continued to plough his arse with long languid strokes. It was all I could do to stop myself from laughing. It was like watching an American porn film; there are times when it's better to do it with the volume turned off. Still, it was enough to keep my orgasm at bay. But not his.

He let out one almighty yell, his arse clenched tight against my cock, his toes curled, he lifted his shoulders off the bed and stared at me through wide eyes, the strain showing on his flushed face. Then he started to shake and pant before his body finally relaxed again. He flopped back onto the bed and closed his eyes thinking it was all over. But I hadn't finished yet. He had to be taught a lesson.

Now that he'd relaxed I could continue to pump his arse with my solid erection. This time his cries were of true pain as I battered his bruised arse muscles. He begged me to stop, but he hadn't had enough yet. I'd come to him for help and he'd forced me to have sex with him. Well, he was damn well going to have sex and I'd stop when I was good and ready.

Eventually he recovered from his post-orgasm tenderness and his arse started to relax again. He was actually starting to enjoy it once more. He always was a horny little bastard. When I looked down at him I realised that although he'd shown all the signs of having a full orgasm, and believe me he hadn't faked that, he hadn't actually ejaculated. Well, he'd better get ready for number two. I grabbed his still erect cock in my fist and squeezed tight. Without any more lubrication than the sweat on my palms I pumped it as hard and as fast as I could.

It wasn't long before I felt his cock swell even more and his arse clench again. His whole body went rigid and I was almost afraid he was going to pass out before his first shot of spunk jetted from his cock. I just kept on pumping and thrusting as his head whipped from side to side and his seed shot all over him. His second orgasm massaged my cock until I couldn't hold back any longer. With one final thrust I unleashed my load deep into his bowels.

That was it. We were both well and truly shagged. I collapsed on top of him in post-coital exhaustion. I was just beginning to think he might have learnt his lesson when he went and spoilt it. 'I love you,' he said. And he meant it.

There I was trying to show him how unenjoyable sex without feeling could be, and he'd loved every minute of it. I couldn't believe it. I just felt used and cheap and dirty. I'd come to Colin for somewhere to stay when I had no-one else to turn to. I thought he'd understand. He was supposed to be a nice guy. He was no better than the others. He just wanted sex. He'd pretend to be all considerate and understanding until he got what he wanted. That's when I decided I'd been unfair on Pete; expecting him to live up to an ideal that just didn't exist.

I waited until Colin fell into a deep sleep and then climbed out of bed. I slipped back into my clothes and left. As I pulled my jacket on something hard in one of the pockets rattled against my hip. I pulled Colin's keys out and tossed them on the table before leaving his flat for good. I wasn't going to make that mistake again.

Chapter Four

PETE

Why me? I wondered as my office door opened and Rick oozed into the room. As my Personal Assistant, Rick often enters my office and I've watched him perform the feat so many times that I can anticipate the reason for his appearance merely by observing his body language. He just cannot control his emotions. If he is about to deliver bad news ('The canteen had run out of tuna salad sandwiches with wholemeal bread so I didn't know what to get you instead') the door opens slowly and his eyes focus somewhere through the window behind me. If he is proud of an achievement ('Here's that file you wanted me to find, you wouldn't believe how much trouble I had tracking it down') the door opens swiftly and he gazes somewhere around the bridge of my nose. If he has a confession to make ('I forgot to tell you that someone phoned at lunchtime and I know it was urgent, but I didn't get his name') the door creaks open and he studies the pattern in the carpet. If he has lost his temper ('Fred in personnel says the other PAs are getting their own parking spaces. Why haven't I?') the door slams open and he glares into my eyes. If he wants sex the door opens and he oozes in. Given that he is quite cute with an athletic build and tends to wear tight clothes which compliment it, you can understand why the latter more than compensates for all his other grand entrances. In point of fact, it is the only reason that he is still employed as my Personal Assistant.

Yes, we have had sex in the past. On more than one occasion, actually. Yes, I do know that it is probably less than ethical, but every manager has a dalliance with his secretary. Yes, I suppose technically it does mean that I am cheating on Tim, but it really does not mean anything. It is just sex. I mean, Rick is not the only one I have recreational sex with. He is just convenient when I am working away from home or having to stay late in the office. Okay, I mean when I *choose* to stay late on the occasions when we are both obviously feeling aroused. I have a very active libido, so in my case that is quite a common occurrence.

This evening was not one of those occasions. There really was work to do. And it had to be finished before the next morning or the company was in danger of losing a very valuable account. When I asked Rick to work late I only meant work. As he so often does, he misinterpreted my meaning and obviously had himself all geared up for pleasure.

Rick closed the door behind himself and sauntered across the room. His eyes never left mine as he slid his backside onto the edge of my desk, reached across, got hold of my tie, pulled me toward him and kissed me. He was trying for a deep, passionate affair, but I did not respond. Not that he noticed of course. I had to actually put my pen down and push him away with my hand on his chest. His solid, deep chest.

Perhaps I did allow my hand to linger a little longer than I should. I suppose I might have accidentally brushed my finger against the hard stud of his nipple. But it was not my intention to lead him on.

I simply told him that we really had work to do and that if

he could not control himself, then perhaps he should forget his overtime and leave me alone to get on with things. He obviously did not believe me. He smiled a knowing smile, raised himself to his feet and unbuttoned his shirt as he cruised around my desk. For one awful moment I thought he was going to plant himself in my lap. Instead he took firm hold of the arms of my chair and swung me round to face him.

One hand grasping each chair arm, he leaned forward so that he totally invaded my personal space. His shirt fell forward so that I could see the soft layer of dark hair covering the globes of his tanned, muscular chest. His rosy nipples just peeked out from inside his crisp white shirt. I pulled my gaze away from them and looked up into his deep blue eyes. He leant closer and breathed into my ear, 'You don't really want me to go.'

At this range the scent of his eau-de-toilette was so overpowering my head started to swim. Any other time he would have been correct about what I wanted. Truth to tell I wanted it then, but it just was not convenient. Tim had made a point of reminding me before I left home that morning that it was our anniversary and he would expect me home at a reasonable hour. He probably had one of his special meals planned. And then I was landed with this problem account which I knew would delay me, but with Rick's extra pair of hands it could still be finished in time for me to be home before Tim came to the boil.

Rick only had one plan for his hands and we were both beginning to simmer nicely, thank you. In an attempt to break the rising mood of eroticism between us I got to my feet. Again Rick misinterpreted this as permission to play. The action had actually brought us closer together physically and he simply folded his arms around my waist while dropping his head to nibble gently at my neck. My head automatically fell to the other side and a soft moan escaped me as his lips clamped down around my pulse. He rubbed his groin into mine and I felt our erections make contact, sensitive, hard flesh sliding over sensitive, hard flesh.

Gathering all of my inner resolve, I managed to pull myself back from the brink of total submission. I pulled my arms free of his embrace, placed my hands firmly on his shoulders and pushed him away. I reiterated my statement that we were here merely to work and that he should put all other ideas out of his head or he would be of no use to me. He merely smiled his heart-stopping smile.

In retrospect it may have been remiss of me to leave my hands on his broad square shoulders while I spoke, but I was preoccupied with the inner conflict attempting to reaffirm priorities. Perhaps I should have broken the eye contact, pulling back from the depth of those bright blue orbs. I should definitely have stopped him from unbuttoning my shirt. I knew things had progressed too far when I felt his warm breath on my chest and his ample lips around my nipple.

I truly felt as if I were a schizophrenic. One of my personalities, the straightforward sensible one, insisted on stopping Rick and getting on with the job at hand so that I could spend a pleasant evening with Tim celebrating our anniversary. A second, the free-wheeling carefree one, hankered after giving in to Rick and indulging in passionate sex here in the office with no regard to the consequences. With some effort I decided to be sensible.

Rick moved on to my other nipple.

A third identity made an attempt to broker peace with a compromise. Just have a quickie with Rick, then get him to help out with the work so that I would be just a little late for Tim. I could make it up to him somehow.

Rick's teeth grazed the edge of my nipple.

My carefree self surrendered, lay back, spread his legs and

raised the white flag. My sensible self responded with an assault on two fronts. Not only would I be disappointing Tim again, but I was also likely to lose the lucrative account by not completing this urgent task. The twin guilt grenades exploded right in Rick's face.

I grabbed a fistful of Rick's sandy floppy hair and pulled, jerking his head back and away from my erogenous zones. 'I told you to stop,' I yelled into his pain-wracked features. 'We have not got time for fooling around. There is a lot of work to be done on this account. This very influential account. This very lucrative account. This account which pays your overinflated salary. The salary which keeps you in designer clothes, a fashionable residence and a sporty little penis extension of a car. I asked you to work late to help me complete this task in time for me to keep a personal engagement this evening. If I want to use you for any other purpose I will let you know. Until then you can just keep your smutty little libido under control and refrain from attempting to take liberties with me in future. Do I make myself clear?' Rick did not answer, but I could see a healthy dose of fear mixed in with the shock and pain in his eyes. It is not normally like me to react so violently. I had been under a lot of pressure both at work where several accounts all called for my personal attention, and at home where Tim was showing signs of unrest. Still, it does no harm to put the help in their place every once in a while and Rick had been letting his performance slip, in all ways, for some time now.

With a final tug I released my grip on his hair. For a brief moment he looked as if he were considering standing his ground to make a fight of it. But even he managed to work out that this would be a mistake and he just turned on his heel and flounced out of the office. I would probably have to tolerate his sulking for a few days, but at the time I had more pressing concerns. I refastened my shirt, sat behind my desk and started to work.

By the time I surfaced from behind the mounds of complex paperwork several hours had passed. I had completed everything that was needed for the next day, but it had taken the whole evening and I had become so involved in the task that I had failed to keep track of the time. I had not even warned Tim that I would be late. I hoped he would be in one of his more understanding moods, although I somehow had my doubts.

When I finally arrived at home an ominous darkness surrounded everything. Ominous because Tim normally waited up for me when I had to work late on special occasions such as this. I began to feel worried when I found the microwave to be empty. On the occasions when Tim retired before I returned he always left a meal prepared for me to reheat; even when he knew I would be late because of a dinner with a client. He said that he worried I was conducting more business than eating at those affairs and he wanted me to keep my strength up. It was ironic that he did not realise he was keeping my strength up for an altogether different type of affair.

When I saw the unwashed dishes in the sink I was close to panic. Tim was so proud of our expensive home that he lavished care and attention on it. He even tidied up after parties as soon as they had finished; no putting things off until the next day for him.

I decided that it was too late to prepare anything to eat for myself. The tricky account and having to deal with Rick had really taken a lot out of me. I arranged my features into my best contrite expression, preparing to weather the approaching storm as I made my way to the bedroom.

As it turned out I was worrying unnecessarily. Tim was

already in bed and apparently sleeping as peacefully as a baby. The comparison to a slumbering child is sound; despite his muscular build Tim has a very powerful aura of innocence and vulnerability about him while he sleeps. It is something that defies description; you just have to experience it. Lulled into a false sense of security, I removed my clothes and slid between the satin sheets.

I was soon made aware that all of my attempts at stealth had been in vain. As soon as my head touched the pillow Tim's eyes flew open, indicating that he had not been asleep at all. The steel behind those hazel eyes did a wonderful job of representing the barricades which Tim manned so ably against my every attempt to apologise. It was clear that he was geared up for a full scale argument. I did not have the energy and was determined to deny him that pleasure. Eventually he stormed out of the room in frustration, leaving the waterbed undulating in his wake.

I could almost understand why Tim should be so upset. I had missed our anniversary, after all, and from the look of the debris in the lounge and kitchen he had prepared one of his special meals. But did he have to be so damn belligerent about it all? He had seemed to be increasingly moody in the recent past. I considered letting him get over it with a night to himself in the spare room, but became concerned that he might just spend the time brooding on things. Pop psychology seemed to be that you should never go to bed on an argument. Not that I ever let other people's thinking influence the way I live my life, but I did have a slight ulterior motive. The business with Rick had affected me more than I would care to admit. I was feeling so aroused that the prospect of spending a night alone between the satin sheets on the waterbed seemed intolerable. If I gave Tim enough time he might calm down enough for a reconciliation.

* * *

I could not say how long I waited. Time drags when you are left to your own devices with raging hormones. I slipped out of the bed and walked carefully to the spare room. Even the deep pile of the carpet seemed to caress the bare skin of my feet in an erotic manner. I stopped at the door and listened for the tell-tale sounds of Tim's rasping snore. When Tim's sinuses are on form his snoring reaches a volume which overpowers the television in the lounge. Tonight it was a mild rattle so I decided it was safe to enter without disturbing him.

Tim was normally a very deep sleeper with nothing short of a minor earthquake being able to rouse him. Perhaps that was how he managed to remain asleep despite his own snoring. Still, I decided not to take any chances. I closed the door carefully, tip-toed across the room, raised the edge of the sheets and edged onto the bed. As it was only a single bed I could not avoid making some contact with Tim, but he was curled up on one side of the bed so I put my back against his and tried to settle down.

It was not long before I felt him shift his position behind me and a large arm wrapped itself around my waist. As usual physical contact with Tim had a pronounced effect on me. I could feel my solid erection growing rapidly. What I did not expect to feel was Tim's hand grasp my cock, give it a firm squeeze and pump it a couple of times. I decided that he must have woken and wanted to work off some of the excess energies of the evening. That was more than fine by me. It was just what my libido needed.

I turned to face him as he released his hold on my member, keeping his arm around me, and our mouths met in a deep and passionate kiss. His tongue batted firmly against mine and his powerful arm crushed me against him. The pre-come was streaming from my aching erection.

Then it all stopped just as suddenly as it had begun.

Tim pulled away from me, turned over and resumed snoring. Had he truly been asleep all the time or was this his perverse idea of punishment? I was too turned on to care. I snuggled into his back, putting my arm around him, and letting my rampant cock throb against the solid mounds of his arse through his underwear. Tim continued to snore. Perhaps some gentle coaxing would restore his amorous mood. I edged closer and began to breathe heavily so that I was effectively blowing on the back of his neck. I gently stroked my hand across his firm stomach. Tim continued to snore. I slowly raised my hand to his bulging chest and ran my fingers lightly over his hard nipples. He grunted slightly but continued to snore. As a last resort I moved my head forward, gently pressing my lips against the back of his neck and pushed forward with my hips pressing my drooling cock harder against his firm buttocks. Even if he stayed asleep I might be able to satisfy my raging hormones.

Tim's snoring stopped.

With a loud yell he knocked my hand away, threw back the covers, leaped out of bed and hit me with a verbal tirade. He proceeded to rant incoherently as he prowled around the room, rummaged through the wardrobe and struggled into some clothes he found there. I watched bemused as his angry monologue reached its finale and he made his exit. Shortly afterwards I heard the front door slam. Once that was all over I pulled the covers back over me and tried once more to settle down to sleep.

Again I was not aware of how much time passed, but it did not feel like long before I was forced to forsake all hope of a good sleep in favour of satisfying the twin desires which raged within me. My cock had been up and down so many times that evening that my balls were starting to ache with the pressure of a heavy load desperate for release. The second ache was deep in the pit of my stomach. I had not eaten since lunchtime and I was beginning to experience the cramps of hunger pangs. With a sigh I dragged myself out of bed, returned to our bedroom, pulled on my tracksuit and trainers and grabbed my car keys and some cash. Pausing in front of the hall mirror just long enough to be sure I looked presentable, I left our home and headed for the nearest place I could think of where I stood a good chance of satisfying both cravings.

I pocketed my change, lifted my tray and looked around for the best place to sit. Even at this late hour the motorway service station was not deserted, but none of the other patrons looked enticing enough for me to use a table near them and attempt to contrive a meeting. Instead I looked for a vacant table with the best position. I was in luck. I found one which provided a clear view of not only the entrance, so I could watch out for prospective talent arriving, but also the cash registers so I could attempt to make eye contact as they paid, and the exit to the toilets for reasons I should not need to explain.

As you would expect, the food was not exactly a gastronomic delight, but I was too hungry to care and the prospect of finally calming my sex drive more than compensated for the cuisine. Not that a shag seemed imminent. Although there was a fair amount of trade passing through, mostly parties of revellers on their way home after a wild night on the town, on the whole my eating companions were pretty grim. I was lingering over my coffee and considering the merits of returning home to a video and a solo session with five good friends when things suddenly improved.

The guy who came crashing into the service station just then was quite stunning. Even if he had not slammed through the door in an obvious temper I would still have noticed him. He was not beautiful, but his mean and moody look perfectly suited his demeanour. I would say he was probably in his mid to late twenties, of average height with what looked like an athletic build, although it was hard to tell through his clothes. He had very dark close-cropped hair. His face was slender with prominent cheekbones, large brown eyes encircled by long, dark lashes, a masculine nose which could have been broken at some time in the distant past, a large mouth with ample lips which probably stayed permanently in that slight pout, and a scattering of dark stubble which added to the shaping of his face and his overall rugged appearance. His clothes also had the look of basic masculinity. Black footwear, which could have been workboots, blue jeans which fitted snugly in all the right places, a plain white T-shirt, which was tight over his torso, or at least what I could see of it beneath his black leather jacket. He was just what my libido had been waiting for and I was drooling all over again.

Having paid for his coffee, he turned from the cashier and looked for somewhere to sit. His dark eyes met mine and paused. I could swear I saw his mouth turn up in a slight smile as he headed for a table directly in front of me. He put his cup on the table and slipped out of his jacket. His body was fantastic. He looked to have none of those bodybuilder bulges through his clothes, just a physique that reflected regular, but careful use: someone who plays sport frequently for enjoyment or has a very physical job. He hung his jacket over the back of the chair and stretched, giving me a perfect view of all that trim muscle. He slid onto his seat and his piercing eyes held mine as he drank. His large, strong hands held the cup quite steady and I noticed that even his nails matched the image: well cared for, but not preened. This time he definitely smiled and I found myself smiling back.

He kept his eyes locked on mine as he put his cup down and moved elegantly out of his seat. He continued to smile as he lifted his jacket from the back of the chair and, in one smooth movement, slung it casually over his shoulder. I shifted my gaze from his eyes just long enough to register the cords of sinew in his forearm, bunched up by the weight of the jacket he held. With a slight nod toward me he turned and strolled off in the direction of the toilets. Now my hormones may have shifted into overdrive, but my brain was not totally out of action. I slowly drained the last of my coffee and glanced discreetly around. The place was virtually empty apart from a group of youths sat in a corner. They appeared to be too deep in conversation amongst themselves to pay any attention to what might be happening around them. Once assured that I was not being observed I stood up and nonchalantly made my way to the gents.

The combined smell of ammonia and urine was incredibly powerful and I felt a slight stinging in my eyes. Carefully glancing around, I moved over to a urinal and began to undo my flies. Presenting the image that I was merely there to pass water I turned my attention to my surroundings. It would have been too obvious to actually look around, so I tried to make use of my other senses instead. The stench was still overpowering my nose, not that I really expected to be able to smell anyone else. The individual urinals were made of porcelain so the flow of urine against them made little noise, but the acoustics were such that all sounds echoed around the vast, empty room.

As I finished emptying my bladder and shook the last rogue drops free I heard the sound of water spraying into a hand basin. Shortly after that stopped I heard the loud hum of a hand dryer. Not wanting to miss my opportunity I quickly put my cock back into my tracksuit bottoms and headed towards the sounds. In my haste I almost collided with someone coming in the opposite direction. Unfortunately it was not the youth I had been trying to follow. It was a much younger, rougher looking, weedy boy. He just sneered at me and pushed his way past. I do not know whether he registered my surprise or not, but he certainly gave me a shock. I became incredibly aware of the risks I was taking by attempting to have a sexual encounter in a public place. It would not be the first time, but on the other occasions I somehow did not think about things quite as much.

I was washing my hands and considering whether the risks were too great to proceed when I heard a creaking noise behind me. I looked up into the mirror and saw a cubicle door swaying slowly. My apprehension regarding the risks was instantly transformed into excitement. I felt my pulse begin to race, my throat constrict and my mouth turn dry. I watched the door open wider to reveal the occupant. It was the youth I had followed, but he looked quite different. I ran my tongue across my parched lips as I admired the sight reflected in the mirror. His leather jacket hung open, framing his powerful torso, one hand forced his T-shirt up to his chest and played with a nipple partially obscured by the material, and his jeans rested half way down his legs, while further up, midway between his chunky thighs and the flat planes of his stomach, his other hand slowly stroked his rising manhood.

I stood transfixed before the mirror for some time. When his member reached a full erection he smiled and backed into the cubicle. The door began to swing shut snapping me out of my trance and convincing me to make a move. Again my tongue darted across my lips and I looked furtively around to make sure I was not observed. Only when I was sure I had not been seen did I give in to the thrill of the possibility and head toward the already occupied cubicle. I slipped through the partially open door and swiftly closed it behind me.

He stood with his back to one side of the cubicle. Still smiling. Still stroking his cock. I moved into position facing him. Keeping his eyes fixed on mine he slowly raised his hand from his cock to his mouth and allowed a long trail of saliva to trickle onto his palm. He worked it around with his fingers before returning his hand to his cock. Hearing the slight slurping sound created by his now lubricated flesh I glanced down. His rigid cock glistened with the coating of saliva and I was fairly sure there was also an ample amount of pre-come mixed in there as well. Seeing my fascination, he stopped his rhythmic stroking and grasped the base of his cock. Maintaining his grip, his fingers edged slowly up his shaft, gathering a fold of skin before them as they reached the head. A small drop of pre-come squeezed out of the slit in his gland and remained balanced precariously at the very tip of that handsome pole. The gathered skin covered the edge of his gland and pulled his sac tight against his balls, pushing them forward. Still entranced, I watched as he let his hand languidly undertake the return journey along his shaft to the base. There he cupped his hand around his balls and squeezed gently. His erect cock throbbed, dislodging the drop of pre-come which trickled slowly along the thick vein at the front of his shaft. The fluid seemed to catch the light like a tiny crystal as it inched tortuously along its route. My eyes followed the progress until the drop collided with his hand and pooled against the edge of his finger. There was a moment of absolute stillness until I became aware that he was watching me, waiting for me to make a move.

I suddenly became very conscious of my lack of participation. In all the time since entering the cubicle I had hardly moved and I was aware that I was still fully clothed. Glancing down I saw my erection straining at the front of my tracksuit bottoms and decided it was time to join in the fun. I hooked my thumbs into my waistband and lowered my bottoms just far enough for the material to hang loosely around my rigid cock. He looked slightly puzzled that I had not dropped them further exposing myself completely. With a knowing smile I joined my hands together forming a hoop which I gently slid along my cock. When I reached the base I pushed my hands closer together gathering the material of my bottoms with them. This left my cock wrapped in the soft warm cotton. I gently rocked my hips back and my cock slid slowly through my hands, leaving the material behind to fall limp in its wake. I rocked forward and my cock re-entered the firm, smooth hole. I was effectively fucking a sheath shaped perfectly to the outside of my cock.

Seeing my ingenuity he smiled and raised an appreciative eyebrow before resuming his own action. Keeping one hand firmly gripping his balls which held his cock rigid in place, he leant his head forward and I saw his cheeks working as if he were chewing gum. Eventually his lips parted as his tongue pushed through to release another stream of saliva which travelled, with expert aim, straight to the centre of the head of his cock. There it rested uneasily until another stream dislodged it so it flowed over the edge of the gland and down the sides of his shaft. He looked smug as he removed his other hand from beneath his T-shirt and spat on his palm. He then coated his whole cock with the saliva. Responding to the treatment his cock throbbed and twitched. When he had finished it stood proud, pink and shining like a bodybuilder covered in baby oil.

Wrapping his fingers loosely around the shaft, he gave his cock several slow, smooth strokes. All this time I continued to hump my tracksuit bottoms. He turned his attention to the edge of his gland, making his strokes shorter and faster. A dark stain grew at the end of my make-shift sheath as my pre-come soaked through the material. He stroked faster. I humped harder, feeling the soft material caress my cock with each thrust. The fibre gently teased my skin while my hands rubbed firm in contrast. A jolt of pleasure shot through my entire nervous system each time the tip of my cock rammed home against the end of the sheath. He stroked even faster. His hand became a blur, concentrating purely on the edge of his gland. His knob was so red it virtually glowed. He closed his eyes and threw his head and shoulders back against the cubicle wall. His whole body looked tense in preparation for his orgasm. I felt my own balls tighten as they too got ready to unleash a load of their own. And then it happened.

With a loud clatter an empty drink can came flying over the cubicle door and caught him a glancing blow to the forehead.

The impending moment of ecstasy was lost as he yelped, more in surprise than pain I thought, and raised his hand to his head. I bit my lip in an attempt to stifle the laugh which threatened to burst free. It was not that I found his misfortune funny. I am not that insensitive. Although the comic timing had been impeccable if you appreciate slapstick humour. I believe it was all the pent-up emotions of the day mixed with the aborted orgasm demanding release in any way it could manage. At that moment hysterical laughter was the most likely option. I think he noticed my discomfort and misinterpreted my motives as his face darkened to a scowl which would have been rather appealing under other circumstances. Unfortunately, at that time, it merely looked comical. I was just on the brink of losing the struggle to contain the hysterics when even that channel of emotional release was also dammed. The earth moved. Almost literally.

From outside the cubicle came so much noise it sounded like a full scale riot was taking place. I could not distinguish any specific words due to the volume and mixture of voices. It was more comparable to animalistic guttural growls and snarls than human language. The similarity to being trapped by a group of wild animals made the whole thing even more frightening. Then, just as suddenly, the noise stopped. Had they been chased away? Had they just got bored and gone of their own accord? Still looking annoyed, my companion reached for the lock on the cubicle door. Instinctively I grabbed his wrist before he could open it. Perhaps they were just trying to lull us into a false sense of security? My nerves on edge I tried to force my mind to work properly instead of giving in to the severe panic it felt more comfortable with just then. Would we have heard footsteps if anyone else had entered the gents or indeed if our tormentors had left? The silence stretched indeterminately.

I was almost convinced that I was being paranoid and loosened my grip on his wrist. Then my suspicions were confirmed. We both leapt into the centre of the cubicle almost colliding with each other as the assault resumed. This time they were pounding on the door and walls of the cubicle as they yelled. The flimsy wood shook ominously, threatening to give way before the onslaught.

If I thought I had been scared earlier that was nothing compared to the absolute fear that gripped my system at that time. Even though we had a strategic advantage (the only way they could get to us was by climbing over the cubicle walls and they did not look sturdy enough to take the weight of a person) we must have been outnumbered. It was also clear that we were susceptible to airborne attack if they could find suitable ammunition. All of this was magnified by the almost subconscious feeling of guilt. What we had been doing was wrong. Sex in a public place. Even worse: sex between men in a public place. The same risk which had added to the excitement of the encounter now reduced the chances of escaping this assault unscathed. Even if the rabble outside were disturbed and dispersed before the cubicle walls collapsed we would probably be discovered and more than likely prosecuted as a result. This sordid little escapade could put my whole career in jeopardy.

Just then the activity ceased. This time I could hear scurrying sounds probably caused by our assailants rushing to adopt an innocent posture. Other cubicle doors slammed closed, water could be heard spraying into sinks and hand dryers roared into life. Obviously I could not hear it, but I was prepared to bet that some people were even standing before mirrors combing their hair. I could only reason that someone else had entered the lavatory, whether drawn by the noise or merely to make use of the facilities. Perhaps the mob would not take the risk of being observed in their activities. It was a slim chance, but one I was prepared to take. I reached for the lock, took a few deep breaths, and opened the door.

I could not tell you what was taking place outside the cubicle. I was too focused to pay any attention to my surroundings. All of my concentration was being utilised to fight my basic instinct to run out of there as fast as I could. My pulse was racing. My mouth was dry. I could feel the perspiration breaking out all over my body. I kept my eyes fixed firmly ahead, but could focus on nothing other than the door to freedom. With great restraint I kept my pace steady as I walked away from the cubicle. At least I believed it was steady. Perhaps I staggered or swayed slightly under the influence of the adrenaline rush. If I did, any observer probably thought I was drunk. It felt as if I had travelled miles before finally reaching the door. I yanked it open and almost jumped through it.

Outside the lavatory I still did not stop. I just wanted to get away from the whole situation as quickly as I could. I quickened my pace in case I had been followed, but tried to remain calm. There were other people around in the service station, so surely I could come to no harm now?

I continued to fight the urge to panic until I reached the car park. The open space seemed to renew the potential danger and I ran to my car, fumbling in my pocket for the keys. My hands shook as I forced the key into the lock and turned it. Suddenly there was a blaring sound of a car horn and lights flashed. I almost jumped out of my skin and prepared to dive behind the body of my car for protection.

It took a few moments to realise that it was my own alarm which was causing the fuss. In my haste I had forgotten to disable it. Embarrassed, I pressed the button which switched it off and slid into the driving seat under cover of the silence and darkness which ensued. My nerves were beginning to steady as I started the engine. Not wishing to attract any more attention to myself, I did not even switch on my headlights until I was leaving the car park and about to rejoin the motorway. I had had more than enough excitement for one night. I was heading straight for home.

Chapter Five

RICK

I don't mind telling you I was furious. Just where did he get off treating me like that? Who does he think he is? He might be my boss, but he's no better than I am. And he's not that great in bed either. I just do it for the perks I can get. But I'm getting ahead of myself.

When Mr High and Mighty Bossman Pete asked me to work late I knew just what he had in mind. Exactly the same thing he had in mind every other time he asked me to work late or accompany him on a weekend business trip. He wanted a shag. Oh, I know. I've heard all the arguments before. About abuse of position and how degrading it is to let the boss have his wicked way with you. It's not like that really. I mean yeah, sure we have sex when it suits him and it doesn't go down too well if I have a headache or a prior engagement, but I'm not in this for love or anything. I just play him along, let him have his jollies and think about what I can get out of him this time. At least he knows better than to try fobbing me off with flowers or chocolates. Please! And costume jewellery is out; if it comes near my skin it has to be genuine. No, I get it through expenses. While we're away we stay in the best rooms and eat at the best restaurants and occasionally we get to see a show, but mostly he countersigns my travel expenses and overtime claims without too much scrutiny. And he has the say on how big a rise I get. Let's just say I've had a few performance bonuses that warranted quite a performance on my part. And don't give me that look. It's not common whoring. And you wouldn't do anything different if you had the chance.

So, back to the plot. We're 'working late', he's already waiting in his office and I'm taking my time about getting ready for him. It always pays to build up the anticipation. You don't want to look too easy. Just what d'you think you're laughing at? Anyway, I'd checked out my hair, making sure it flopped just right above my eyes, loosened my collar a little, done a few isometric exercises to get that bit of a pump in my muscles and liberally squirted the Jean-Paul Gaultier EDT I keep in my desk drawer just for these occasions. Yes, it is rather too expensive to 'squirt liberally', but I'd managed to charm the full range out of him for my birthday the other month. I know my birthday's not for another few months. It's just that he has such a bad memory. If I play it just right I manage at least two birthdays a year, like any good queen. But, stop interrupting or I'll never get to the juicy bit.

I figure he's panting for it by now and I'm working out which shade to buy that little Ben Sherman number in as I make my entrance. No, nothing like that. He's into butch (if you don't fucking stop laughing I'll slap you!) and I'm into the money so I manage to act the part. He's sat behind his desk, shuffling papers as he does trying to impress me with his 'I'm so important' routine, but it doesn't wash. Once you've seen someone in the throes of a premature ejaculation, face all red and sweaty and scrunched up, they lose all delusions of grandeur they may try for later. He's not too important to beg to have his arse fucked, either.

So, shoulders back, chest out, hips forward, I swagger across the room to his desk. I plonk my luscious arse on the edge, lean across, grab him by the tie, pull him forward and land a juicy smacker right on his gob. He pretends to be surprised and look startled, but he's a crap actor. He reaches forward and makes a show of pushing me away with his hand on my chest. I flex my tits a little and he moves his hand slightly so his fingers rub against my nipple. Toying with my joystud, he tells me there's work to be done and perhaps I should leave him alone. So now I know we're into the role-play scenario. I'm to be the wicked temptress who interrupts his hard evening at the office and seduces him into shagging me senseless across the desk. I can go for that. You should see the roles we've played out alone in hotel rooms; this was much more tame.

Anyway, I take a moment to get into character before sliding off his desk, letting his tie slip through my fingers. I slowly unbutton my shirt as I manoeuvre around the desk to where he's sitting. He just watches, his eyes fixed on the firm torso I'm tantalisingly revealing. When I reach him I grab hold of the arms of his executive chair and swing him round to face me properly. Overwhelmed by the passion, he sits back in the leather chair as I lean forward and exude sex from every pore. My shirt falls open and he takes the opportunity to get a good eyeful of my fit, tanned body. I can see the lust in his eyes when he drags them back up to meet mine. I let mine smoulder for a moment before leaning further forward to whisper sweet nothings in his ear.

That does it. He practically leaps to his feet and lunges at me. I close my arms around his waist and pull him to me while bending forward to nibble at his neck. He gives up all pretence of resistance and leans his head to one side while I lap and suck gently at the side of his neck. Not too hard, mind. I have to be careful not to leave a mark. I don't know why he's so paranoid about that. It's not as if it'll be a permanent scar or even if anyone else is likely to notice it. He seems to be such a sad loner that you'd expect him to be proud of the fact someone got close enough to give him a mark. Mind you, if he showed it off like a trophy people would probably think he did it himself. He moans softly and pushes his groin into mine. Twisting his hips, he rubs his erection against my own hardening cock.

Suddenly Pete slips back into character. He wriggles his arms free, puts his hands on my broad shoulders and makes another half-hearted attempt to push me away. He needed to put more effort into his dialogue as well. He just repeats his earlier monologue about how we had to work instead of playing. I decide to stick to a silent role and merely smile back as he rubs his hands over the solid muscle of my shoulders and gazes into my eyes. Following the direction of his body rather than his words, I unbutton his shirt and smile my best evil seductress smile before sinking to clamp my mouth around his tiny nipple.

I feel him tense as I let my tongue play with the little stud. I roll it around the edge and then flick it a few times before sucking the surrounding flesh past my lips and pressing it against the roof of my mouth. I let it spring free and move across his pigeon chest to his other nipple, taking a moment to prise the stringy chest hair from between my teeth. Then my tongue repeats its award-winning performance to the audience on this side of the house. This time I don't settle for sucking, but also throw in a minor ad-lib with my teeth. It's not as if I bit down properly. I know some guys who love that. I just grazed it lightly. It certainly wasn't enough to warrant him kicking off the way he did.

He grabs a fistful of my hair and yanks back, almost pulling it out at the root. Then he's in my face. Yelling and screaming as if I've committed some mortal sin. Something about how I shouldn't be behaving like that and how he reckons he owns me 'cause I owe him so much. At first I think he's still fooling, but I'm not into the rough stuff and the pain in my scalp feels as if I'm in danger of acquiring a bald patch. He gives my hair one more tug, as if to prove a point and then lets go. I hesitate for a moment, wondering what my next move should be. This most definitely wasn't in the script. He just stands there. I figure I don't care whether he's still playing or not. If he wants to behave like that he can go back to solo performances. I turn and storm out of his poxy office.

I tell you, I'm so steamed I almost decide to jack the whole job in. Nobody treats me like that and gets away with it. But then I figure that he'd probably think he'd won if I do that. So instead I decide he can just whistle for his little sexscapades. I don't need the extra cash as much as he needs the relief. No, I think the best way to get my own back is to carry on at the office and let him see just what he can't have any more. And if he does want it again it'll cost him big time.

No, that's not all there is to it. It gets worse. Having finished with that prick Pete, I figure I need to work some of the tension out of my system so I drive over to the gym. I'd got my kit with me anyway because I normally end the day with a quick workout, but that pillock had really screwed things up for me. When he'd asked me to 'work late' I'd phoned my training partner and told him I couldn't go. By the time I arrived he'd already been and gone, so I had to go through my routine on my own. Mind you, it was probably better that way because I was still in a foul temper. I just focused on my exercises and worked out that aggression. I was so focused I didn't even take the usual time to ogle the other talent and you know that's not like me. I usually have trouble keeping my eyes off all those mountains of masculinity, pumped-up muscles bulging and covered in sweat as they strain to gain another fraction of an inch. It always has a profound effect on me and I have no trouble gaining plenty of inches. That's why I wear such baggy shorts while I'm there.

Anyway, as I said, that night I'm so focused I don't know what's going on around me. I don't notice the time at all. I'd arrived late enough, but by the time I've finished my workout it's getting close to closing time. I figure I just have time for a quick shower before heading home. The warmth of the water helps to ease the rest of the tension from my body as well as some of the ache from the muscles I'd worked. It's so relaxing I'm tempted to stay longer, but I'm now very conscious of the time. I finish scrubbing myself down, turn the water off, and start to towel myself off as I stroll into the changing room. That's when I realise I'm not alone.

Mack, the owner, is sitting on the bench next to my clothes. Now, I think Mack is the most gorgeous man in the world. He's not a competition bodybuilder himself, like so many other gym owners are, but he is incredibly fit. He is the absolute epitome of masculinity. His body is full of muscles which bulge from regular activity without looking inflated from overpumping and he's always wearing tight or skimpy clothes which show it off to its full advantage. Tonight he's straining inside a khaki vest and purple cords. He's also tanned a deep even brown, suggesting regular trips to the sun rather than the solarium. His features are ruggedly handsome, with stubble which just looks unkempt rather than designer and it's all topped off with jet black hair which flops forward into his eyes. He's just sitting there, feet stretched out in front of him, head back, leaning against the wall. His hands are clasped behind his head, which causes his biceps to bulge and his forearms to strain. His eyes are closed and I'm half convinced he's asleep until he speaks.

'Not working on the tan tonight?' he asks as I try to

manoeuvre the towel around my middle without drawing attention to the instant hard-on he's given me. Just his voice alone is enough to get me worked up. It's deep and masculine with a broad local accent. 'No, I figured it was getting too late and you'd want to close up,' I reply, still unable to look him in the eye and fairly certain I can feel a flush of embarrassment in my cheeks. 'That's okay,' he says with a smile, 'I don't mind staying late for special customers. Finish drying off and I'll see you round there.' With that he gets up and saunters out of the changing room. Even his walk is macho. I can't stop myself from gazing at his tight buttocks inside his trousers as he leaves. Was I imagining it or was there something more in that smile? I'm sure he noticed the prominent bulge behind my towel. Perhaps this evening won't be so bad after all.

As fast as I am, by the time I reach the solarium Mack's nowhere in sight. There's just a token on the counter with a pair of goggles. I leave the money in exchange for the token and head for the tanning room. I'm still wearing my towel from force of habit. Even though it's a men-only gym and it's fairly mixed I still don't feel comfortable flashing my cock to everyone. Well, not in surroundings like that anyway. I leave my towel on a hook in the wall, put the goggles over my eyes, stand between the fluorescent tubes and slip the token into the slot. With a slight hum the tubes spring to life and it's not long before I can feel the heat searing through my skin. This is the other thing that eases the muscles I've been straining during my workout. Trying for an even tan, I've got my arms stretched out at my sides. It's a huge walk-in tanner so there's plenty of room. I let my mind wander and an image of Mack brings my cock back to life. I figure it's better to be tanned with a hard on so that gets to be an even brown as well.

The heat seems to be increasing and I can feel the sweat breaking out all over my body. I'm sure it's not usually this hot. Suddenly there's a click and the room's plunged into darkness. Now, I'm sure I've not lost track of time again and it's just the end of my session. Besides the overhead lights are out too. With my goggles on it's like being in total darkness. 'Sorry about this, mate.' I nearly jump out of my fucking skin. 'The power's just packed up.' It's Mack's voice from just the other side of the tanner. And it's getting closer. 'I'll give you a free session next time to make up for it. In the meantime I thought you might like to try this. It's a new product just arrived. It's supposed to really bring out the tan without giving it that orange hue. It's also supposed to be really good for the skin, helping to prevent the cancers everyone whinges about. And that power surge just before everything cut out might have overdone you a bit.'

Now I'm starting to worry. I mean it's one thing to try for a healthy tan to match the fit body, but it's another to risk getting cancer. I'd always thought the reports were just scaremongering and Mack had always reassured me before. It's hard to distrust someone who looks like that. I didn't stop to wonder why I hadn't heard the door open or why Mack had entered the room instead of calling from outside. I wasn't wondering much about anything when I felt him join me in the tanner. I can't think of anything at all when I hear the pop of the container opening and the sound of the solution being spread on his strong hands. I can feel his body just behind me and I breathe in sharply as his powerful arms reach round my sides and his firm fingers begin to massage the liquid into my taught stomach. The sensation of the cool liquid against my skin, still hot from the tanner, is amazing.

I lean back as his hands work their way slowly up to my solid chest. I feel the wiry hair of his chest prickle against my shoulders before I reach the solid muscle of his pecs. His rounded biceps are rubbing forcefully against my sides while his hands continue to work. When his fingers graze my nipples I groan loudly and throw my head back onto his shoulder. His hands are starting to dry out and I feel them run down my body once more. When they reach my lower abdomen they stop and I just can't help myself. My cock jerks with pleasure and leaps up until it hits against the back of his fingers. Instinctively I push back with my hips until my arse reaches his groin. And I'm not disappointed by what I find there. It feels as if his cock matches the rest of his body perfectly. It's long, thick and rock hard. It's so thick it's spreading my cheeks just by pushing against them.

Mack gives a little laugh and slides his hands onto my hips. Then he twists me round so I'm facing him. I still can't see a thing in those damn goggles, but I'm too worked up to think about that. I just lean forward to kiss him.

Suddenly his hands are on my shoulders. He's applying increasing pressure until he's forced me down on my knees. Startled I'm looking up where he should be, still unable to see. He lets go with one hand and I can hear the rasp of a zip which can only be his flies opening. Then his remaining hand clamps harder onto my shoulder. The fingers digging into the tender muscle until I cry out in pain. But before I can finish my cry I'm gagged by his huge cock. I feel the head push past my lips and straight to the back of my throat where it stops briefly, blocked by my constricting muscles. Then both his hands grasp the back of my head and push me forward as his muscular legs push his hips into my face until his cock has forced its way down my throat and my face is pressed hard against his groin.

His huge cock is so wide that my jaw is stretched to its limit and my throat is completely blocked. I'm in danger of suffocating and starting to choke when he pulls out just as forcefully, leaving the head of his cock resting on my lips. I'm gagging and coughing up bile at the same time I'm gasping and trying to swallow air. I'm still convulsing when he thrusts back into me as deep as before. Now there's no way I can fight back. My body's wracked by spasms as it struggles for breath and to eject the blockage. And he's so big I'm stretched too taught to even try to bite. I don't know why he's being so forceful. I'd gladly have given him a more luxurious blow-job if he'd only asked. I'd been gagging for it for ages. Yes, I know, poor choice of words.

Anyway, he's settled into a steady rhythm now. And my system has almost managed to match it so I'm feeling less discomfort and actually managing to breathe after a fashion. His thrusts are still just as forceful, but my throat's starting to get numb to the battering. Then he pushes in with one particularly deep lunge and doesn't withdraw. I'm so busy fighting for breath that I'm only vaguely aware of one of his hands leaving my shoulders and reaching behind me. It slides down the small of my back and along the crack between my buttocks until it finds the hole beneath. I try to gasp as a wide finger pushes against the lips of my hole, but I only manage to swallow his cock even further.

My sphincter clamps down against the intruding digit, but it's just as powerful as the rest of him and it soon forces its way past until it's sunk in right up to the webbing of his fingers. There it wriggles around until it hits my prostate and I try for a groan which is also stifled by his cock. The finger pulls out, back to its first knuckle and then it's joined by a second. Together they force their way past my surrendering sphincter. When they are sunk completely inside he forces them apart and twists them around. I can feel them rubbing against the insides of my bowels. Then, still spread wide, he yanks them out completely painfully stretching the ring of my arse. I lose the last of my breath in an attempted cry of pain which only manages to be a smothered gurgle. I'm going light-headed from the lack of oxygen and my vision is starting to go even darker at the edges.

I'm on the verge of passing out when he pulls his cock out of my mouth. I don't even have the energy to gasp. I just breathe deeply, feeling the oxygen burn against my battered throat and lungs. I offer no resistance as his hands slide into my armpits and he hoists me to my feet. He spins me round away from him and pushes me forward so I'm leaning against the warm tubes of the tanner, his hands on my hips. By the time my brain recovers enough to realise what he's about to do it's too late. With a single thrust he buries his huge cock in my arse right up to the hilt. I scream in agony as I feel the edge of my arsehole tear and my insides bludgeoned into pulp. He's gone way past my prostate and squashed that to one side so I'm not getting any pleasure from this. My whole being is focused on the excruciating pain in my bowels as he roughly withdraws and plunges back into me, trying to find a rhythm which suits him.

Totally defeated, I'm like a rag doll. He's holding me up by my hips as he ploughs into my sore arse. I don't know how long it goes on for. It feels like forever. I'm not even sure if I passed out for a few moments from the pain. All I know is that I'm almost totally numb in my arse by the time I vaguely hear his breath getting laboured and he starts to shout and growl so I guess he's coming. I don't actually feel him withdraw, I just find myself dropped on the floor where I curl up into a ball and hope to be left alone. That's when the power comes back on and the tanner springs back into life. Isn't that quite a coincidence!

The timer sounds and the tanner clicks off again before my strength starts to crawl back. I struggle to my feet and sway slightly as my vision blurs, waiting for the blood to find its way back to my head. As I recover my senses I notice I've still got an erection. I can't believe I actually got off on being treated like that. I suppose it's not technically rape as I was willing to have sex with him and I didn't get a chance to refuse to do anything. The way my cock is standing to attention I'm not sure I would have refused anyway. I've never known it to get so hard. I'm still feeling abused and determined that he won't get away with it, but he's much bigger than me, yes all over, and I don't want to go to the police so I did the only thing left to me. I have a wank.

Closing my eyes, I picture him making love to me the way it should have been. His stubble chafes my lips as he kisses me deeply and with passion. His hands caress my body tenderly as he crushes me to him in a longing embrace. When his huge cock enters me it is with care and compassion. Yes, it still hurts, but he takes it slowly, allowing me to adjust to the discomfort before gently thrusting in a soothing rhythm which rocks my whole body from my prostate upwards. He looks down at me lovingly, holding back his own orgasm until he knows I can't stand this pleasure any more. With a deep cry of passion I shoot the biggest load of my life. The sperm flies through the air and just pumps and pumps and pumps until I can't stay standing anymore.

When I recover from that orgasm I grab my towel and walk out. You know the bastard had even wiped the blood and grime from his cock on my towel? In the changing room I rush into enough clothes to make myself decent and race out of there.

How was that getting revenge? Well, when I came I shot all over his fucking tanner. It'll take some doing to clean that lot from behind his tubes.

Chapter Six

MACK

Yeah, sure I did it. So what? They were asking for it. These queers deserve whatever they get. Prancing around like girlies. Giving men a bad name. I mean, no-one cares what people do in private. But that's not enough for those queers. They want to be treated like respectable people. They don't want to behave respectable, though. And they won't stick to their own pubs and clubs. Oh no. They have to try to infiltrate everywhere. Like a disease. And don't get me started on diseases. Gay plague. Hah!

Some of them have even joined the gym I run. Time was when it was a respectable place where a man could go to work out with other men. Sure we'd admire each other from time to time. That's the point of all the work we're putting into these bodies. And so what if there's some fooling around in the showers. It don't mean nothing. It's just high spirits. And there are times when a man's just got to help out his mate 'cause he needs a little special treatment. Like when his woman isn't playing ball. Or when he just wants that thing he can't get from a woman. It don't make him any less a man.

But these queers are taking things too far. They're spoiling

71

it for the rest of us. They're trying to look like real men, but they act like girls. There's this one in particular. Rick. A real queer if ever there was one. He likes to grunt and groan when he's working out, like he's being real hard, but he only ever lifts sissy weights. He's too busy batting his eyelids at all the other men. And he's forever coming on to us. He just won't take no for an answer. Just 'cause some of his kind giggle and fool around in the shower with him, he thinks we're all available. Well, he's wrong and this night I decided to let him know it.

At first I think he's not coming in. His fairy partner's already been and gone through his little routine. I notice he's quiet, though, and keeps himself to himself without Rick to goad him on. I'm just tidying up in the weight room and thinking about closing a bit early when Rick swans in as if he owns the place. He's like that. He always looks down his nose at you like you're a piece of dirt or something. Hah, he's not even that good. So he's there farting about with those prissy weights of his and all the time he's staring at me in the mirror. He thinks I don't notice, but I can feel those fairy eyes undressing me and gazing at my body. I try glaring back at him to let him know his attention's not welcome, but he just goes on leering.

I decide to leave him to it and head off to my office. I'm pottering around in there when I hear the showers running and start to think. Why should I lock myself away in there? It's not like I'm the one in the wrong. I bet he's in the shower now soaping up his feeble dick and dreaming about what it'd be like to have a real man like me. I know he wants it. I've seen the way the front of his shorts stretches when I'm around. Maybe I'll let him know what he's missing. Let him have a taste of what a real man's like. He won't want it again by the time I'm through with him.

By the time he's finished preening himself in the shower I'm in the changing rooms waiting for him. As soon as he sees me his little prick jumps to life. He tries to cover it with his towel thinking I haven't noticed, but he's too late. I sweet talk him into having a session in the walk-in tanning machine. I make it sound like I'm doing him a favour and I can tell he's taken the bait hoping for more. I walk out of there and go to set my trap.

I take a bottle of cheap sun lotion and leave a token and a pair of goggles on the counter, then hide in the room with the tanner. I'm crouched down on the floor behind the machine by the thermostat and fuses so he doesn't see me when he minces into the room. He's humming away to himself as he hangs up his towel and steps into the machine. Humming one of his poofy show tunes I bet. I turn away as he starts the machine, keeping my eyes protected. I give him a little while to settle in and then I turn up the thermostat. Real slow so he won't notice until he's cooking away. When it reaches a point where I can almost smell the fairy toasting I pull the fuse and everything shuts down.

I can smell his fear from where I'm hiding. He's practically wetting himself. He almost has a heart attack when I speak to him. I calm him down, making an excuse about a power surge. A real man would know it's not true, but these queers know nothing about mechanical things. I join him in the machine. I want to make him think he's going to get what he wants from me so I act all nice. I offer to use the lotion on him and he's actually panting with desire. I pour some onto my hands and make like he's a girl. As soon as I touch him he's groaning and playing up to me. He leans back onto my chest as I rub my hands on his tits. When I tweak his nipples he's in seventh heaven. He throws his head back onto my shoulder and moans. For an instant I almost find myself thinking that he is a girl and slide my hands down his smooth sides toward his fanny. I'm even starting to get turned on myself. Then he reminds me he's supposed to be a man as his tiny prick springs up and eagerly rubs against the back of my hand. But he shows me he wants to be treated like a girl by pushing his arse into my crotch and rubbing at it until he gets me all worked up. I bet he's never felt anything that size before. He's sliding his arsehole up and down my cock like he's desperate for it. But he's not getting it yet. At least not there. I laugh at the thought of what I'm going to do to him. I grab his girly hips and roughly twist him round to face me. The pervert actually tries to kiss me. I am going to enjoy teaching him a lesson.

I grab hold of his shoulders in a grip like a vice to make sure he won't try any more sissy stuff. He thinks he's fit just 'cause he plays around with a few light weights. Hah. He's a real pushover. It takes hardly any effort at all to push him down onto his knees where he belongs. He's looking up at me like a slave adoring his master or maybe even a religious fanatic worshipping his God. Yeah, he's a fanatic all right. And I know what he's worshipping. He's staring right at the huge bulge in my trousers. He's licking his lips, he wants it so much. My cock's straining at the leash as I think about the pain I'm going to inflict on him. It's like a wild animal desperate to ravage its prey. And it's not going to be held back for long.

He's such a wimp I can keep him in his place using only one hand. With the other I unzip my fly and pull my huge cock out of my trousers. I turn the hand on his shoulder into a claw and dig my strong fingers into his soft, wimpy flesh. His face is all screwed up as if he's in agony. That really turns me on. I squeeze a little harder just for the hell of it as my cock reaches its full rock hard state. If he thinks he's hurting now he's in for a real surprise. He's crying like a baby and it's getting on my nerves so I shut him up. I shove my big cock in his gob and keep pushing 'til it won't go any further. I'm sure he's used to sucking cock, but I bet he's never had anything as big as mine before. I'm not exaggerating here. I've seen quite a few men around in the showers at my gym and not one of them has ever come close to being in my league. Even women have trouble taking it all. They usually whinge about how much it's hurting before it's even half in. But I know they love it really. Just like Rick's going to love it when he gets it all. Right up until he's begging me to stop 'cause he can't take the pain and pleasure any more. He's nowhere near halfway down at the moment and his puny throat is trying to fight back. It's no contest. I just link my hands at the back of his head and pull it toward me as I push forward with my hips. I can feel his throat stretch as my knob pushes past and slides right down his gullet. I keep pulling until his face is squashed against my groin.

I just hold him there for a little while, enjoying the feeling of power I have over him. I bet I could crack his head like an egg if I squeezed hard enough. But I decide to go easy on him. I just pull his face into me until his nose is pressed flat against me. I bet he's really enjoying my manly smell down there. Or he would be if he could breathe. My cock is plugging his throat and my groin is blocking his nose. I can feel him squirming, but he doesn't stand a chance. His throat is working wonders on my cock as he starts to choke. His face is turning red and he looks in danger of passing out, so I give him a break and yank my cock back out as far as his lips. I want him to stay conscious so he can feel what's happening to him. He's gasping and gagging and sounds as if he's about to puke. I don't want that kind of mess in my tanning room, and it'd put me off, so I figure he needs to be plugged again. I shove my huge cock back down his throat. All his coughing and spluttering must have greased it up a bit 'cause it slides down much easier this time.

The more his throat struggles against my cock the better it feels. It squeezes against my big knob and sends shivers right up my spine. I guess my basic sex drive takes over as I start to thrust in and out of his warm hole, getting a regular movement going while I fuck his face. I close my eyes and enjoy the way the feeling of pleasure spreads through my whole body. I'm really getting into it when I realise he is too. I don't know how but he's managing to breathe somehow and his throat is starting to relax. It just doesn't feel as good without the same pressure. And he doesn't look in as much pain. Maybe I've worked this hole enough. Maybe it's time to move on to his other end. I shove my cock as hard as I can as deep as it'll go to keep him busy while I explore.

I bet his arse is real loose from all the fucking he's had. It still won't be loose enough for me, though. I move one hand down to his arse and feel around until I find his hole. I don't like touching him there, but past experience has taught me I have to. Too many times I've tried fucking someone without stretching them a bit first and sometimes it's just so painful that I lose my erection before I even get in properly. And I want him to feel the power of the whole thing. I push my middle finger into his hole and he tries to fight back again. He should have learnt by now that he's no match for me. And I know he really wants it 'cause his throat is now pulling my cock even deeper down. I just shove my finger as far as it'll go into his tight hole. Shit, it feels like you could fit a whole bus in there once you get past the ring. It feels like the poof's really starting to enjoy this. He's groaning and moaning like a bitch in heat. He might think he wants it now, but I know better. He'll soon change his mind.

I pull my finger out far enough for my index finger to join it. Then I push them both back in together. He's not even trying to fight back this time. I open my fingers wide and twist them in his guts. He's still making happy gurgling noises. But not for long. I just want to stretch him enough to make sure I can get my battering ram in there without too much trouble. Keeping my fingers apart I yank them back out of his hole. He didn't like that as much. It must have been like passing the biggest shit of his life. And it's going to get bigger.

He's starting to go limp down there on his knees. I don't know if it's the pain causing him to pass out or if he's suffocating. I don't really care as long as he stays with it long enough for the finale. I pull my cock out of his face and he doesn't move. He doesn't even close his mouth. My cock is glistening with a thick coating of drool and it's dribbling out of his open mouth too. I think I'm going to have to slap him a bit to wake him up, but his eyes are still open and he's still breathing. He'll get enough of a jolt in a moment.

I grab him under his arms and drag him to his feet. He just hangs there limp, not even trying to support himself. He's mine to use as I want. And I'm going to. I spin him round and push his shoulders forward. His arms raise automatically so his hands rest on the tubes of the tanning machine. I move my hands to his hips and pull back until his arse is in the air. His hole is lined up perfectly with my huge knob. His feet barely touch the floor so I'm still supporting him and in total control of his body. I press my knob against his hole to make sure the angle's just right and shove. Suddenly he's not so limp anymore. But it's too late. I'm so fucking hard and he's so worked over that a single thrust shoves my entire mammoth cock into his arse. I can feel his ring trying to clamp down on me, but I'm just too big for it and it tears under the strain. He's screaming fit to burst and lashing out with his hands. Finally he grips the tubes and holds on for grim death. He's getting the ride of his life. His head's thrashing back and forth as I steadily pump in and out. His hole's nice and hot and his struggles make it tight against my cock. I'm really getting into this when he starts to loosen up. He's going all limp again so I figure I need to finish off quick. I speed up my thrusts and drive in to the hilt with each lunge. I can feel the pressure building in my balls as they slap against his quivering arse. I'm feeling nothing now except the hot sensations of lust and pleasure in my cock. It's swelling even bigger. I'm not even trying to hold back. I shove myself as far into him as I can and start to unleash my heavy load. My whole body is shaking with the force of my orgasm, which seems to last forever.

When I come down again, he's just hanging limply from my softening cock. I'm still holding him up by the hips. I've been holding so tight you can see bruises starting to form on his sides. I bet he's got a few bruises on the inside too. I lift him off my cock and drop him to the ground. I've no use for him anymore and he'll know better than to consider messing with me in future. As he's lying there I notice his little prick's still hard. Maybe he enjoyed it after all. Maybe he'll be back for more. Maybe I'll give it to him if he's real nice.

I leave him lying still on the floor in a pool of sweat and push the fuse back in before leaving. As I open the door I see the state my cock's in. It's covered by his filth and blood. The dirty queer. Well, maybe he won't be up to anything for a while until he heals properly. I wipe myself clean on his towel and head for the showers.

I stay in the shower in my office until I feel I've washed his filth from my body. Then I stay in my office until I hear the main door close. I don't even want to dirty my eyes with him at the moment. I go into the tanning room to shut everything down properly and that's when I see what the filthy little bastard's done. The little toe-rag must have enjoyed it 'cause he couldn't stop himself from having a wank. I bet he was dreaming about my huge cock pounding his insides as he shot his feeble load. But the little git had shot inside the tubes of the tanning machine. That'd take some cleaning out. He'd better not show his face in my gym again or I'll show him what I'm like when I'm really playing rough.

Chapter Seven

CARL

Huh, it turned out to be a better night than I'd thought. 'Specially after that one looked as if 'e'd got away and trashed my bike in the bargain. What one? Oh yeah, I've not told you about 'im yet, 'ave I?

It's a Friday night and me and the gang are on the prowl as usual. We've 'ad a few drinks and a few laughs in the local bikers' club. We're supposed to be barred from there, but them bouncers are just wimps. Not one of 'em stands up to me when I get started. So we're well tanked up and the club closes. It's been a quiet night without any fights at all. Maybe they all know me too well in there now, but no-one reacts when I try to start anything. We're all in need of some kind of action so I say we go and try some poof bashing. Now there's two places to find poofs round 'ere on a Friday night. One's in their pubs and clubs, but we don't go near there. The police have got the area well patrolled. The other's in the bogs where they go for a quick shag. That's where we normally go. You can make quite a sport of it. And we'd be world champs.

The best place we've found is the local services on the motorway. We can sit around in there for ages and no-one tries to move us on, while we wait for a likely looking poof to turn up. Then we send the Kid in as bait. We send the Kid 'cause 'e's the pretty one and everyone knows poofs go for 'em young and cute-looking. When 'e's got 'em all interested 'e persuades 'em to take 'im somewhere quiet and deserted. Then we turn up and beat the crap out of the poof. What's 'e going to say? If 'e tries anything we say the Kid's underage and 'e's my little brother. I've got a right to protect my brother, 'aven't I?

So we're sat there in a corner joking around over a couple of drinks between us and nobody even glances in our direction. It's funny 'ow people don't see what scares 'em. Then this likely-looking target comes in. 'E's wearing one of those designer track suits and fair reeks of money. And class. The way 'e carries 'is tray all careful like and slides into 'is seat. Yeah, 'e looks like a poof. And a rich poof at that. Now we've spotted our prey, we wait. It's not usually long before the victim traps 'imself, wandering into the bogs to see what's on offer. Then we get 'im and give 'im more than 'e bargained for.

It looks like we're in for a long wait this night. The guy just sits there brooding over 'is food. When 'e's finished eating 'e nurses 'is coffee and keeps eyeing everyone who arrives. That's all 'e does. Just watches 'em all. Never makes a move on any of 'em. I decide it's time to unleash the secret weapon and send the Kid to get more drinks and see if 'e can get the guy's attention while 'e's there. Just as 'e's going into 'is best 'elpless routine things start to liven up. This other guy comes crashing into the place. 'E's definitely wound up about something. Everyone stares at 'im, 'e's made such a racket coming in. But our guy's still staring at 'im after everyone else 'as gone back to eating and drinking. We could be in luck. We might get two for the price of one.

I catch the Kid's wrist and get 'im to wait a bit before starting 'is act. The new guy looks round a bit as if it's a hard choice where to sit. The place is damn near deserted. Then 'e settles for a table right in front of our guy. Now, the posh one 'asn't taken 'is eyes off the new guy even for a second. 'Is face is a picture. 'E's just sat there with 'is mouth open and staring while the new guy makes a performance of taking 'is jacket off and stretching for 'im. Now we've done this long enough to know the signs. The new guy's on the game and 'e's spotted our guy for a punter. 'E's a real pro and 'e's got 'im trapped quicker than the Kid could do. The signals are obvious between 'em. It won't be long now before we can join in and get both of 'em.

The rent boy finishes 'is coffee, gets up, slings 'is jacket over 'is shoulder and heads for the bogs. The posh poof hesitates. I'm sure 'e's going to follow. 'E just wants to make sure it don't look too obvious. Well, 'e's too late for that. I let go of the Kid's arm and signal 'im to follow the prostitute into the bogs. 'E scoots off and we wait, watching the posh one. 'E's still trying to look calm and casual, but it don't work. You can see 'is nerves shaking from 'ere. 'E 'as a shifty look round and then 'e heads for the bogs too. Now we just wait. There's two ways this can go. Maybe the Kid's already made contact with the prostitute and can lure 'im out for us to deal with, but I'm hoping for better things. If the Kid's as good as I think 'e is 'e'll just bide 'is time to see how we can get both those guys at once.

Sure enough, it's not long before the Kid comes back to us with a grin all over 'is face. 'E says the first guy in the bogs is definitely on the game and shows us this note with 'is price on it. 'E's not cheap. Our guy definitely looks like 'e can afford it, though, and the Kid reckons 'e's up for it too. But 'e says 'e looked so edgy that it'll take a while for 'im to get down to it and they might do it right there in the bogs. So the plan's changed, but I like to think I'm adaptable. I'm just not quite sure what to do for the best yet. Do we wait and follow one of the guys when 'e comes out until we get a chance to mug 'im and do 'im over? Or do we go for broke and catch them at it so we can do 'em both? I decide to wait for a bit and see what happens.

Now I can be real patient, but the other guys are getting restless and it's been a long night. Neither of the poofs shows any sign of coming out, so I decide it's time for Plan B. It's risky doing it right here, but if it comes off it'll be worth it. We head for the bogs. Not all at the same time. That'd be too obvious. I told you we're masters at this game. Leaving Jez by the door as lookout, we take up position around the trap they're in and listen for a bit. It don't sound as if they're doing anything too heavy, but from the grunts and gasps I'd say someone's close to shooting. Wouldn't it just be a shame if something 'appened to spoil their fun?

With a quick look to make sure everyone's ready I lob my empty can over the door. There's a soft thud and a yell so I guess my aim was better than I'd hoped. The noises in the trap have definitely changed so it's time to let 'em know how much trouble they're in. I signal the gang and we start yelling and shouting like we're at a football riot. When I decide we've done enough to panic 'em and flush 'em out I give the signal to stop and everything's quiet again. I give 'em a few moments but it looks as if they're not coming out yet. Time for the next stage. At my signal everyone starts shaking and banging at the trap walls and door. If they don't come out soon we're likely to break through.

Then Jez dashes in to let us know we're about to be interrupted. It all goes like clockwork. Everyone knows what they're supposed to do. The guys in the traps either side of our target go further in, slam the doors and lock them. The few left outside start to wash their hands and I stand outside the door of the trap with our prey inside just in case they try to make a bolt for it, looking for all the world as if I'm just waiting to use the bog. I told you we were good. By the time the guy walks in everything looks normal and 'e doesn't even give us a glance as 'e walks over to the urinals to have a slash.

Now this is where good planning shows. One of our targets decides to make a run for it while things are quiet. It's the posh one, I thought it would be 'cause 'e'd looked nervy from the start. The guys near the door look at me to see if they should stop 'im or follow, but I just shake my head slightly. We've still got the real perv trapped. And to make sure 'e stays trapped I slip into the trap before 'e can get any ideas. To the visitor it just looks as if I'm taking my turn to use the bog and that I'm rushing 'cause I'm desperate. I'm desperate all right. Desperate to make sure we don't lose both poofs. The one in the trap's startled and before 'e gets any big ideas of making a fuss, I've got 'im pinned against the wall with me 'and over 'is mouth and me blade poking in 'is ribs. I'm giving 'im the eye so 'e knows I mean business. It's not long before Jez sounds the all clear and I know the fun can really start.

Chapter Eight

MIKE

The cold night air did nothing to cool my temper. I was still fuming when I arrived at the motorway service station, even after the walk from Colin's flat. Perhaps that was why I hadn't pulled before reaching the main building. On a good night I don't make it across the car park without being approached. Hell, on a really good night a passing car stops me before I reach the service station grounds. I don't think my anger had put them all off, some of them really go for a mean-looking guy, but I was so wound up I wasn't paying much attention to what was going on around me. I probably wouldn't have even noticed if a punter had stopped right next to me and waved his wallet in the air. Anyway the cold had started to get to me through my leather jacket. I don't generally feel the cold easily, another result of spending so much time walking draughty streets between open street corners or prowling round open park spaces. I suppose the underground canal walkway is covered, but even there the wind could pass straight through you if your punter didn't have anywhere else to take you. So the chill's beginning to reach my bones and I decide a hot drink's in order.

Now, I realise just how bad a mood I'm in when the door crashes against the wall when I open it. Only the most dedicated masochist could be into someone that irate, so I decide to try to calm down. When I reach the counter I seriously consider ordering decaf, but I figure I need a treat so splash out on the best filter coffee they have. I unleash my best charming grin on the cashier and she fairly falls off her stool she's so bowled over. I swear I could hear her drool puddling on the floor beneath the counter. So I figure I've mastered my temper and not lost my touch and look for a table. Normally I would have to settle down at a table and draw out the time spent drinking the one cup of coffee (that's where flirting with the staff helps, they're less inclined to throw you out if they fancy you) while waiting for my prey to arrive, but this time I was in luck. As soon as I looked up I saw this guy gazing back at me. I could almost feel the waves of lust radiating from behind those eyes. I can tell he's already hooked, but I figure I'll show him the bait anyway. Put on a bit of a show. My ego could do with the strokes after this evening's fiasco.

I stroll straight to a table in front of him and slide my tray onto it. I ease first one shoulder then the other out of my jacket and let gravity pull it down my arms. I've practised this move so often I can do it in my sleep. I catch the jacket by the collar with one hand and swing it round to rest on the back of the chair. Having demonstrated my dexterity and suppleness it's time to give him a view of the goods. I let him have my most effective stretch. My hands go to the back of my neck so the biceps bulge against the sleeves of my T-shirt. My head drops to one side and I rotate my shoulders back which pushes my chest way out in front. Arching my back slightly not only pulls my stomach in it also pushes my pelvis forward, giving a clear view of my crotch. All this stretching lasts for exactly ten seconds before I sit down and busy myself with the coffee.

I can tell from his expression that he's taken all this in and he's definitely interested, but I don't want to risk being complacent. Some guys show they're totally into you, but are too scared to follow through and approach. Approaching them is just enough to push them over the edge and they run like scared rabbits. I don't need any more rejections tonight so I keep feeding him morsels of eye contact while trying to read him. After all this time in the business I'm really good at this. He hasn't got that look of desperation about him that I see in those who are just too shy to go for what they want. And he's not ugly enough to be the kind who normally have to pay to get anyone half-decent to touch them. I don't do them anyway. I have my standards. Well, okay, only when times are really hard and they only get the economy service and at inflated rates. No, this guy has the look of a businessman about him. He's dressed casually, but in designer gear. Is he so career-minded that he can't be bothered forming relationships so he goes out cruising when he wants sex? Nah, he'd probably have a harem of secretaries for that or use one of the high-class up-market escorts or a gentleman's club. Perhaps he's straight and only dabbles occasionally? Could be. He's not wearing a wedding ring, but very few do when they're on the pull. I decide he's the sort of person who knows what he wants and how to get it when he wants it so I don't need to play around any more.

Smiling to seal the deal, I put my cup down and start to get up from the table. His eyes follow mine as I rise. I retrieve my jacket and sling it over my shoulder. He keeps looking at my body as if it's doing some kind of act for him, but doesn't move to follow suit. I figure he's okay with it, just making sure we aren't clocked. I'm not sure how he thinks anyone could have avoided noticing the attention he'd paid so far, but let him keep his delusions as I turn and head for the loo. He still doesn't follow, but I swear I can feel his eyes gazing at my behind.

A quick glance round confirms the loos to be unoccupied. It doesn't do to waste time in these situations so I head straight for a stall and leave the door ajar. I hear the main door open shortly after I've entered, so I'm sure I've timed it right and he can see where I'm going. I hear the footsteps approach, but they don't follow me, instead they head off into the stall next door. I check the wall for any holes that he might be planning to use, but there aren't any. I doubt that he has a portable drill with him so I wait for his next move. It's not long in coming, but it's a total surprise. A piece of paper pushed under the stall wall with a few words scrawled on it. 'How much for a shag?' it says. Well, I start to wonder if it's a set-up, but I know the cops aren't allowed to be the first to suggest paying for sex so I decide to play along. I put my jacket back on so I can reach the inside pocket where I keep my pen; handy for giving out contact numbers for future business. I add my price and return the note.

When I hear the stall door open and close again I begin to get myself ready for his entrance. I unbutton my jeans and pull my T-shirt free of the waistband and up over my washboard abs. But he still doesn't arrive. I begin to wonder if he's been put off by the price when I hear water running in the sink followed by the hand dryer coming to life. Perhaps he's just fussy about cleanliness? Then I think I can make out a second pair of footsteps so he's probably just killing time until he can enter unseen. I wait until I hear the main door open and close, but still he doesn't make an appearance. When I hear the water running again I figure he needs some gentle encouragement. I open the stall door a fraction and look round to make sure I haven't made a mistake. But no, it's definitely him standing at the sink. I get myself into position and pull the door further open. I can see his eyes staring into the mirror taking in the whole scene. I've pulled my jeans partway down and am holding my T-shirt up giving him a tantalising glimpse of the firm flesh underneath. He licks his lips in anticipation when he sees my other hand slowly working my cock into life. From the look on his face I could tell he liked what he saw, but he still didn't move. I didn't feel like taking the risk of putting on a performance where it could be overlooked by anyone who entered the loos so I retreated into the stall and let the door close. If he didn't follow through now, then nothing would get him to.

I had no worries there. He was so keen he virtually dashed into the stall before the door had a chance to close properly. At least he had the sense to close and lock it behind him. I'd already moved to one side to make sure he could get into the stall without any trouble, but he still didn't show any signs of getting closer. He just stood there watching with that goofy look on his face. Perhaps he was just into watching? Or perhaps I hadn't warmed him up enough yet. So I go into my 'show them what you've got and let them decide what to do with it' routine. I lift my hand up to my mouth and spit on it. Not just a quick gob. A slow, sensual drool. That kind of shows my dominant side. Trouble is, the spit tends to slip through your fingers so you have to wriggle your hand about to keep hold of it. Then I rub it all over my cock. This makes it shine in the light so it looks even bigger, not that it's not big enough anyway, it just kind of makes it more of a focal point. So I stroke it gently. See if that tempts him to reach out and take over. He's just standing there licking his lips. So now it's decision time. I can see he's fixated on my cock, but where does he want it? I grab hold of my balls and squeeze so my cock swells to its full size and point it at him. The next move's his. Does he drop to his knees and wrap his mouth around it? Does he drop his pants, swing round and sit on it? Does he even reach across and grab hold of it? Does he, fuck.

I mean, I know the guy's turned on. He's got a raging boner poking through his jogging pants. But he just stands there staring. As if he's under a spell. Maybe I'd figured him wrong, I thought. Maybe he hasn't done this before. Then suddenly he snaps out of it. He grabs the waist of his bottoms and starts to lower them. I figure he wants a fuck and I'm just about to reach in my pocket for the condoms when he stops again. Now I haven't a clue what's going on. Nothing's coming off, that's for sure. Then he does this thing with his hands so his cock's wrapped up in the cloth of his pants. And, with this goofy look on his face, he starts to hump his clothes. I've seen some things in my time, but it was all I could do to stop myself from laughing. He looked so comical holding the front of his pants and wriggling his body about. Sort of like a toddler who's just stopped wearing nappies and has wet himself. Still, it was his money. If he just wanted a communal wank that's what I'd give him. But I was in the mood for something more, really, so I'd give him a good show and get it over with as quickly as possible.

While he wiggled about he was still staring at my cock, so I figured I'd show him a trick I'd developed. Keeping tight hold of my balls kept my cock steady, pointing straight up at me. I worked up a healthy gobful of spit, leant forward and let it drool down toward my cock. Now this is something you can copy at home and I'd practised a few times, so my aim's pretty good. In fact it's excellent. It landed smack on the bullseye, right on my cockslit. His face was a real picture. He stood hypnotised, watching the spit slide down the sides of my cock. He was so stunned he stopped wobbling for a moment. I didn't want that. It would delay things even more so I decided to give him a prompt. Still holding my balls in one hand I spat on the other and slowly spread the spit all over my cock so it was nice and slippy. I didn't want too much friction yet or I might end up coming before him. I gave a few slow strokes of my cock and he suddenly remembers what he's there for and starts to wriggle again.

It might have looked comical, but it obviously worked for him. There was a nice dark stain spreading across his pants where his cock was drooling. He's starting to look flushed, whether from the effort of rocking or because he's near to coming I'm not sure, but I figure I can help him over the edge. I rubbed faster and kept to the head of my cock, but made sure my grip was loose so I wasn't getting too close myself. He responded, wobbling faster and pulling faces as his tension mounted. He was looking even funnier so I had to close my eyes and concentrate on not laughing out loud. I made it look like part of the act by throwing my head back and tensing up. If you time it right, sometimes looking as if you're close to coming brings the other person off even quicker. Then you stop while they're recovering and they don't even notice that you've saved your load for some other time.

Anyway I'm acting enough to deserve an Oscar when something hits me on the head. At first I think it's this guy, miffed 'cause I'm not looking at him. But he seems just as startled. Then I notice the beer can rocking on the toilet cistern. I reach to my head to check out the damage. It's throbbing like mad. When I look at my fingers there's a little blood there so I'm at least grazed. Slightly stunned I look up and the little bastard's smiling. I don't know why he thinks it's so funny, and I'm just about to show him why he shouldn't when all Hell breaks loose.

There's all this shouting and yelling outside the stall. I can't make it out properly but I'm sure I can hear lots of insulting names being used. I look at the other guy and he's quaking in his designer boots. For some reason they stop shouting and I decide I've had enough. I rise to the challenge and reach for the lock to open the door. I don't care how many of them there are I'll soon show them the error of their ways. I know how to look after myself. I need to. But no, he's too scared. He grabs my wrist and I can see his hand shaking. Then I notice I'm shaking too, but I'm not scared, I'm shaking with anger and frustration. Anger and frustration that's about to be turned on him if he doesn't let go of me. He sees my mood and is about to back off when it's too late. There's an almighty crashing as they start to pound on the walls and door of the stall. It's so sudden it even makes me jump. I figure they aren't stupid enough to start climbing over the walls where I can pick them off one at a time using leverage to yank them off and gravity to do them damage. I also figure they think we're surrounded and easy pickings. Mind you we could be if they start lobbing anything else over the walls. The best thing to do is to charge out of the door and lay into them while they're spread out around the stall. By the time the others have come out of the neighbouring stalls the ones out front'll be history. Then it all stops. Just as sudden as it started.

At first I hear sounds of people rushing about, and then just the usual sounds of the loos; water running in sinks, hand dryers blaring, stall doors closing. Perhaps someone had come in to disturb them. I was just working out the best plan of action when Wimpo turns tail and runs. Not even a word of warning. He just unlocks the door and bolts for it. I don't get the chance to follow. I'm still stood there looking shocked when some other guy shoves his way into the stall before the door has even closed. Taken by surprise, I've let him get the drop on me, and before I know what's going on, I'm pushed up against the stall wall with his hand over my mouth and something pointed pushing into my stomach. He doesn't say a word, but his eyes say it all for him. They aren't too clear so he's probably drunk or high, but there's pure hatred in there. This is obviously one of the guys who had been causing all the racket. And at a guess I'd say he's the ringleader.

I hear footsteps getting quieter outside. A few moments later there's a soft call of 'all clear' and the thug smiles. He still doesn't say anything, but he really doesn't have to. That smile is pure evil.

Chapter Nine

COLIN

It didn't take me long to struggle through the initial feeling of betrayal. After all I was getting quite used to it by now. Although I still felt a little numb. Perhaps it was shock. Or perhaps I was keeping my emotions in check so I could get through it in one piece. Either way I felt reasonably calm as I strolled to the bathroom to inspect the damage. The water hadn't actually escaped the bath. All I had heard was the sound of it pouring through the overflow system. I turned off the taps and left it alone to settle back to a reasonable level.

In the kitchen I returned Tim's keys to their place in a drawer and gathered together the necessary items for a luxuriously healing soak in the bath. I took the matches from the drawer (they were next to Tim's keys), an ash tray from the open unit and an eye-mask from the fridge where it was chilling. I took the portable handset from the phone in the lounge (just in case). I stopped in the hall to select a suitable cassette tape from the unit there before heading to the bathroom to pamper myself.

After the last time Tim had walked out of my life I had made a concerted effort to improve things. I was fed up with just coasting along. How could I expect anyone to fall in love and stay with me if I wasn't content with my own life? I had decided to redecorate the bathroom. Hey, I had to start somewhere. Truth to tell, the wallpaper had been already starting to peel off because of all the steam. I'd planned to decorate for months and had new units stored away in the spare room for the best part of a year before actually doing anything. I had gathered up all my resolve and gone out to buy new wallpaper and everything you need to decorate (it was the first time since I'd moved into the flat, so I didn't even have a paste brush). I took a week off work, borrowed a paste table and set to it. I had needed the entire week, but eventually it looked really classy and relaxing. Mind you, the old bathroom fittings were still knocking around in the spare room and there were a couple of small patches of paper waiting to be stuck down again. Even so, I was really proud of myself. And today I was going to take the full benefit of all my hard work.

I slipped the cassette into the player (a battery-operated personal stereo with portable speakers connected), started it playing, lit the candles, opened the packet containing the eye-mask, left it in easy reach (next to the phone) and gently eased into the steaming water of the bath. Even though I say so myself, I think I'd done a bloody good job of turning my bathroom into a place where you can totally relax. The soothing sounds from the stereo were soporific. The floating candles on the iron frames produced a warming glow. A glow which caught in the gently rotating crystals hanging above the candles. The facets of the crystals fractured the light into myriad tiny rainbows on the frosted glass of the window. The regular movement of the rainbows was quite hypnotic. While those sensations calmed my emotions, the heat of the water and the aromatic vapours of the herbal bath foam drained what was left of the tensions from my body. There was just one more thing to do before I could release myself to oblivion. I reached over the side of the bath and took the eye-mask from its packet. Taking care not to drop it into the water I unfolded it, closed my eyes and moulded the soft material around them. The chilled therapeutic liquid it was soaked in gently seeped out of the mask and into the tender flesh around my eyes. The scent of the witch hazel mingled with that of the bath foam. I lay back and let myself go.

I don't know how long I spent in that semi-unconscious state before I became aware of the change in the music. What had been soothing was now sensual, with a breathy voice murmuring about various hedonistic pleasures. My subconscious must have noticed the effect first as I had a full erection. I began to sway, causing a slight current in the water. The liquid simultaneously enveloped and caressed my manhood. I let my mind wander to form a mental stimulus to match my current state of arousal. The first image was of the semi-naked pictures on my bathroom walls. They featured lifeguards on beaches with the surf crashing about their heavily muscled and tanned bodies. But they were too tame and I lack the imagination to enhance the erotic content. Next was a vision of Tim reproducing our earlier sexual encounter. That was still too painful. I settled for the guy I met at the club last night. What was his name? Mike? Yes, he was perfect.

I pictured him as I had first seen him, dancing at the club. Even fully clothed he was an impressive sight. The tight jeans and T-shirt, which hugged his frame and emphasised his musculature. His big brown eyes, which seemed to catch the flashing lights. His bright white smile between moist, kissable lips. Then I was on the dance floor with him, reliving our first encounter. Holding his body to me as we gyrated with the music. But it wasn't the usual swift club music. It was the slow sensual music of my bathroom stereo. I writhed in the bath as

we twisted and turned on the dance floor. The water caressing
the parts of my body which his rubbed against as we moved.
Then he was as I had encountered him in the lounge. Lying
naked on the couch. Lost in a fantasy, stroking his erect cock.
No, he wasn't lost in a fantasy. He was looking across the room
at me. Smiling lasciviously while he worked his member. Now
he was standing in front of the couch, his erection pointing
straight out in my direction. His muscular body glistened with
sweat. He looked at me through hooded eyes as he licked his
lips and approached. Somehow my clothes had also
disappeared. My arousal showed in my nakedness. He was so
close now I could smell his scent. His herbal aftershave or
deodorant. He reached forward and grasped my aching cock.
It was already moist and slippery. His hand glided over the
tender skin. Our mouths met in a passionate kiss. He pushed
me back against the door and continued to grope me. My cock
was responding to his ministrations. He knew exactly where to
increase his grip. Which parts were most sensitive. When to
increase his speed. I felt my balls churn and the pressure build
up all along my shaft. The head felt as if it would explode with
the force increasing behind it. I clenched my teeth, held my
breath and every muscle in my body contracted in a powerful
orgasm. The ejaculate pumped from my cock and met the
resistance of the bathwater. It was like coming in someone's
mouth: the warmth and the pressure didn't ease until I couldn't
bear it any more and raised my hips to lift my throbbing cock
out of the water. The last remnant of semen crawled out of my
crack and oozed down my shaft. Totally spent, I let go of my
member and gave myself over once more to the relaxing effect
of the warm bathwater, soothing music, and soft aromas.

I must have fallen asleep because I remember having this
really strange dream. It was really vivid. I can still remember it
now. I was running through this forest. I didn't know why I

was running. Whether I was trying to escape from someone or something, or whether I was chasing after someone or something, I couldn't tell. I just knew I had to keep running. The forest was dark and very dense and I kept stumbling over tree roots. I was panting for breath and my legs were turning to rubber, but I knew I couldn't stop or something terrible would happen. The forest was getting denser and branches kept whipping across me. I had to slow to a walk to force my way through the foliage. I was scratched and sore, but I couldn't stop. Then I heard someone cry out and stopped to look round, but there was nothing there. Literally. I was stood at the edge of a cliff. I swayed precariously and took a half step back to regain my balance. Again I heard the cry for help. It came from beneath me. I looked down at my feet and there was a pair of hands clinging to the edge of the cliff. I looked over the edge and there was Tim hanging on like grim death.

He just looked up at me with those beautiful eyes of his, pleading with me to help him. I didn't hesitate for a moment. I just dropped to the ground and lay flat, reaching over the edge to grab his forearms. But it was no good. I wasn't strong enough to pull him to safety. Then he started to pull himself up, slowly climbing up my arms. His fingers were digging into my flesh and I cried out in pain, but I held firm. He was as far as my shoulders now and the weight of his body was pushing my face into the ground. I just stayed as still as I could so that he wouldn't lose his grip. When he grabbed my belt I felt myself start to slip and scrabbled for a handhold myself. Just when I thought we were both lost, Tim reached the top and rolled off me onto solid ground.

Neither of us moved for a few moments. We just lay there panting with exhaustion. Then there was another voice. We both looked up and there was Pete. Whether he'd been there all the time I don't know. Tim was obviously pleased to see him and he sprang to his feet and they embraced each other passionately. As I started to get to my feet I felt the ground beneath me start to crumble. I called out as I slipped over the edge and scrabbled for a grip in the loose soil. Either they didn't hear me or they didn't care, because they just stood there kissing each other as I found myself falling. Falling into a bottomless abyss.

I was startled awake by the sudden ring of the phone. I jumped and lost my balance so that I slid under the water. Pulling myself back up to safety, I fought to get the water out of my eyes and nostrils. I grabbed for a towel to dry my hands before reaching for the phone. The ring seemed to become more determined. Would it be Tim ringing to explain why he had to dash off so quickly he had forgotten his keys? Would it be Mike ringing to let me explain about last night and arrange to meet up later?

It was Steven. He was only on a quick break so couldn't explain properly, but thought I should get over there right away. Too startled to argue, I agreed and he hung up before I had the chance to question him at all. Steven worked at the local hospital. If I remembered correctly he was in the Accident and Emergency ward at the moment. Why did he need me? Had something happened to Tim after he left the flat? Was he all right? What could I do to help? What would I need to take with me? Once I stopped panicking I decided the best thing to do would be to dry off, get dressed and drive over there to find out.

Chapter Ten

STEVEN

There was nothing particularly special about the night they met. Although I suppose it was a bit like that old Sandra Bullock movie. It was just like any other Friday night in Casualty. We were just coming out of our busy period. The time shortly after the clubs have closed and the drunks decide it's a good idea to drive home instead of queuing for a taxi, or to hit someone with a bottle because they're sure they deserve it, or to try something highly intelligent like walking on a wall when their sense of balance is completely shot. If you ask me I think some of them should be shot. Oh, I've nothing against people having a good time, or getting drunk, or high, and I know accidents happen. I just think some people should be more aware of the results of their actions on other people. But that's not what I'm supposed to be telling you about, is it?

It was coming toward the end of my shift and, like I said, we'd been busy. I was just winding down when the paramedics wheeled in this guy who was in quite a bad way. He was bleeding from a head wound and was completely unconscious. He looked as if he'd been knocked about a bit and we were worried about concussion. While the medical staff worked to patch him up I took his details from the paramedics. He'd been found in this state on the floor of the gents in a motorway service station. Nobody there knew who he was or what had happened. Given the state he was in the paramedics hadn't stopped to ask too many questions, but rushed him straight here. They got another call so it became my job to register the guy and notify the police if necessary.

To be honest, this is the part of my job I actually like. I get to play detective to some degree. I was given the jacket he'd been wearing to search for clues, but there weren't many. Just enough. The total contents of his pockets ran to a packet of condoms and lube, two pens and a crumpled piece of card. Now adding the condom and lube to the place he'd been found suggested he was on the game or at least cottaging. From the look of his injuries he'd probably picked on the wrong punter and been queer-bashed. One of the pens didn't look quite right. It had the wrong feel to it. When I took the top off I realised why. There was no nib, but a needle instead. It was the kind of 'pen' used by diabetics to test their blood-sugar levels. I rushed to tell the medical staff in case he'd had a hypo and was slipping into a coma. They could try to balance his insulin levels and bring him round.

Pleased with myself, I returned to my desk and turned my attention to the piece of card. Perhaps he'd snatched it from his attacker during a scuffle? Feeling like a regular Miss Marple, I smoothed it out and couldn't believe what I saw printed on there. It was one of Colin's calling cards. Now, I know Colin's not capable of hurting anyone like that. And he wouldn't abandon anyone in that state, either. At least not if he had any choice. I had a sudden vision of Colin chasing off the attackers only to find himself set upon outside the service station. He could be lying there now in a pool of his own blood. I was about to call the police when sanity returned. There could have been any number of reasons why this guy had Colin's card and I don't think either would have thanked me for getting the police involved unless it was absolutely necessary. If the guy had been queer-bashed I might be implicating Colin. I had another vision of Colin behind bars with violent criminals and brutal warders. Okay, I'm a Drama Queen, so sue me. I decided the best thing to do was to try Colin's home number first to see if he was there.

When he answered the phone I just couldn't help myself. 'Thank God you're all right.' I gushed. He sounded sleepy and I'd probably just woken him up. I made sure he realised it was me and that I was at work before telling him to get his arse over here as fast as he could. Then I put the phone down and got on with work. I was still feeling pleased with myself. I just love a bit of intrigue, don't you?

Colin arrived so fast he must have broken every speed limit on the way. The patient had been stabilised and admitted onto a ward, for observation I thought. I took Colin straight up to the ward, acting as mysterious as I could. When we got there I bustled him into the room and stood back to watch the drama unfold. It was a bit of an anticlimax, really. Colin just looked at me as if he didn't know what was going on. I had a look and realised things were worse than I'd expected. The guy was still unconscious and it didn't look as if he'd be going anywhere for a while. Both arms were in plaster, his chest was strapped up, his head was bandaged and what you could see of his face was quite badly battered and swollen. Even his mother would have been hard pressed to recognise him.

With as much dramatic effect as I could manage, I produced exhibit A – the crumpled calling card – and told Colin where it was found. He took a closer look at the guy. Slowly recognition dawned and his maternal instincts kicked in. He wanted to know what had happened, how much damage had been done and what he could do to help. He wasn't very forthcoming with information, just saying the guy was a friend of his, so I wasn't going to get any scandal and gossip there. I took him to see the duty sister, who was reluctant to give any information herself when Colin admitted he wasn't a relative and didn't know much about the guy either, but I managed to smooth things over and she explained the extent of his injuries. Apparently they couldn't be sure until he regained consciousness, but they thought he looked a lot worse than he really was. His insulin level seemed to be balanced so he should be coming round fairly soon and then they could check for concussion.

I tried to explain to Colin that there was nothing he could do and that he shouldn't even get involved if he didn't know the guy that well, but he'd switched into total 'mother-hen' mode. Nothing I could do would drag him away from that hospital until he knew the guy was all right. I even tried to entice him away with the news that I was going out with some friends after my shift for a quick drink at one of the all-night clubs. He was having none of it and was already trying to work out what he could do to make the guy's stay more pleasant. When I left, Colin was rummaging through the magazines at the kiosk and looked as if he'd bought up the florist's entire stock.

The visit to the club wasn't that successful. Most of the people there had already spent the evening and night in other pubs and clubs getting smashed, so they were totally off their faces. Not the sort of environment to be in when you are sober and we didn't feel like playing catch-up. So we decided to just get something to eat and call it a night. We were stood on a corner eating our take-away fried chicken when someone had the bright idea of a trip down the local cruising area. As the weather was cold and the canal walkway was sheltered and we were still rather hyper from the shift, we didn't really want to go home yet, so it seemed like a good idea at the time.

Now don't get the wrong idea. I don't go cruising down there regularly, but I'd heard tales of what goes on, and on the few occasions I'd been there I found the whole environment rather exciting. I don't know quite what the feeling stemmed from. Maybe it was the isolation. The whole place is enclosed and so you feel separated from the real world. It's also been left to go rather to ruin so the rubble and makeshift shelters give a feeling of some kind of desolation. It's probably more to do with the fact that there are always people prowling around in the caged area making it quite clear why they're there. Whatever the reason, under the right circumstances, it's one hell of a horny environment.

Horny, yes. Safe, not necessarily. You didn't know who you would meet down there. It could be an undercover policeman or a potential murderer. Maybe that added to the excitement for some people, but it just scared me. I know there are ways of reducing the risks, but the whole atmosphere is so sexually charged that you aren't always thinking with anything other than your libido. And that's what happened to me that night.

My friends were old hands at the cruising etiquette and nothing fazed them. One stopped to chat to some guys by the bars of the cage while the other went for a wander inside. I stayed outside feeling nervous. And cold. I was about to suggest leaving when I saw them arrive. They obviously knew what they were doing because they just walked straight into the cage and walked off behind the concrete pillars. From the brief view I had as they passed, one of them had looked absolutely gorgeous. Like I said it was cold, but the guy was only wearing a khaki vest and purple cords. He was obviously hard. And he looked it. The vest was stretched tight over a muscular torso and his arms bulged as he walked. His chest entered the cage a few moments before the rest of him and his prominent nipples pointed the way. I hadn't really seen his features, but I had an impression of stubble and black, floppy hair. I didn't take much notice of the other guy. Entranced, I left my friend and wandered into the cage following the route he had taken.

It didn't take me long to track him down. It's not a big area, but all the pillars and alcoves make it seem larger on the inside. He was stood against a wall behind a concrete overhang so he was only visible from the neck down. And that view was well worth seeing. I was getting turned on just from the atmosphere and looking at that incredible body. Then I started to think logically. Well, sort of. He hadn't arrived alone so maybe he had already copped off and they had come here for want of somewhere else to go to be together. But the body language was wrong for that. They were stood side by side and there was too much space between them. The alternative was for them to be in an open relationship or maybe just close friends who were out cruising for a threesome. Not a prospect that appealed to me, but if it was the only way to get to him I'd consider it. If the other guy looked okay. I couldn't remember. Then they made a move. Without a word they split up and headed in separate directions. Maybe they weren't 'together' after all. I knew which one I wanted to follow. And like a lost lamb I did.

I was only slightly deterred by the fact that he walked straight past me without even glancing in my direction. There was still a chance if he didn't cop off with anyone else, or maybe he hadn't even noticed me. I dutifully followed him round a corner to an area I'd never visited before. As I turned the corner I noticed he'd stopped, but it would be too obvious if I did the same so I carried on and stopped a bit further on. When I turned back I realised he still hadn't seen me. His attention was fixed on something else. Something going on against the wall between us. I shifted my position so I could see as well, and what a sight it was. No wonder they were in an obscured corner.

Three guys were really going at it. Two were stood at either end of the wall with the third, prone on his back, suspended between them. They were holding him completely off the ground. He had his head thrown back so he could suck the cock and balls of the guy who held his shoulders. While the guy who held his hips was returning the favour. It didn't look very comfortable to me, but they were certainly enjoying it. So was the guy I had followed. His attention was focused on the scene in front of him while his hand absent-mindedly stroked an enormous bulge at his crotch. Just then the floorshow decided to up the ante. In an amazing show of dexterity, the guy holding the other's hips managed to pull the guy's trousers down to his knees and adjust his hold without dropping him so that he had a clear shot at his arse. The guy who was suspended was still busy with the third guy's cock when he groaned with satisfaction as the other penetrated him with no effort. I also noticed he hadn't used any protection either. Now that was taking the thrills a risk too far. I looked up to see what the object of my passion thought of this. He looked uncertain too. Although perhaps not for the same reasons. He still stood mesmerised by the action going down before him. The hand at his crotch was now squeezing an ample mound of flesh which fair strained at his flies. His other hand reached out to tentatively stroke the buttock of the guy doing the fucking. The guy didn't even miss a stroke. When he didn't get any response, my guy pulled his eyes away and turned to walk back in the direction he had come from.

I figured I might stand a chance now that he was so turned

on and decided to follow him again. Mind you, I didn't want to look desperate so I didn't use the same route. Instead I made my way around the other side of the wall and past the pillars so that our paths should cross as if by accident. They did. And he still didn't look in my direction. I stopped in the same area he did and leant casually against the wall facing him. I tried not to stare too hard while making my interest clear, not an easy trick. With a smile he made a move in my direction. Success at last? It was not to be.

He was walking in my direction, but not towards me. Instead he carried on to a younger, fitter, slimmer blond guy stood further along the wall. The blond said something and they both looked my way before the other snorted derisively and returned his attention to his new conquest. I figured that if I couldn't have it at least I could watch. He just stood impassive staring at the younger guy who reached forward and ran his hands over his solid chest. He leant to kiss the dark-haired guy, but he turned his head away so the blond only connected with his neck. The guy took the hint and turned his attention elsewhere. He slid his hands down the other guy's muscular frame until he reached the groin, where he massaged the huge bulge. Even I could see his eyes widen and his full lips part in an expression partly of surprise and partly of desire. He wasted no time in undoing the dark-haired guy's trousers and sliding them down his massive thighs. Freed from its constraints, an enormous cock sprang out from a nest of dark pubic hair. It really was gargantuan. It looked as if it would reach as high as the guy's navel and about as thick as the younger guy's wrists. And it didn't even seem to be fully erect yet.

The blond guy dropped to his knees and started to worship that cock. He started at the balls and lovingly kissed his way along the still lengthening shaft. The dark guy still stood impassively, sneering down at the younger guy as he licked around the head of his cock. Although it looked to me as if the blond was doing a good job of giving him head, he seemed to be getting impatient. He grabbed the guy by the head and pushed his cock into his mouth. The blond did his best to deep throat the massive member, but it was just too big and he'd been taken unawares. The force of the thrust knocked him back and he lost his balance, falling against the wall. The other guy released his hold and helped him to his feet. He also pulled his trousers up, covering his cock, and fastened them enough so he could walk. He put his arm round the younger guy, and with only a quick glance in my direction, led him off towards a ramp in another corner.

I wasn't stupid enough to try following them up there, but from where I stood I could just see the top of the ramp and there was already someone up there. I couldn't be sure, but I thought it was the guy who'd arrived with the dark-haired one. Sure enough, when they reached the top he greeted them and they exchanged a few words before getting back down to it. Both he and the dark-haired guy opened their trousers and the young blond dropped to his knees once more to begin sucking their cocks alternately. This went on for a few moments until the dark-haired guy shifted his position so that the young blond was on the ground between them. I recalled the earlier threesome scene and decided I'd seen enough.

I turned away and looked for the guys I'd come with before heading home. I couldn't find them anywhere, so I decided to give up and made my way toward the cage entrance. I was nearly out when I noticed someone leaning against the wall looking in my direction. And he was really cute. He was dressed in classic faded blue jeans, white T-shirt and black leather jacket. He looked a little taller than me, slim and a bit younger. His long, thick sandy hair, cut in a fringe which flopped over his brow, gave his features a youthful student look. The neatly-trimmed goatee added enough to the age of his face to stop him looking like a minor.

I turned and leant against the bars while I tried to work out whether he was really interested in me or just looking in my direction. I risked a quick smile and he grinned back, his deep blue eyes fixed on mine. That was a relief, but I still wasn't sure what to do next. Remember, I don't make a habit of cruising down here. In fact I'd never met anyone down here before. I hesitated for some time before strolling over to lean on the wall near him. Not too close in case I looked too needy, but close enough for me to look at him to make sure he knew I was interested. Fortunately, he was bold enough to take matters into his own hands instead of waiting for me to get my act together. With another smile he moved in front of me, leant forward and planted a solid passionate kiss on my lips. Without hesitation I opened my mouth and kissed back, his goatee prickling sensuously against my lips.

After a few moments we parted and stood smiling at each other, holding each other by the hips. I saw my passion reflected in his eyes, so I lifted him off the ground, twisted him around so his back was against the wall and took him in another lustful embrace. As our tongues jostled together, mingling saliva, our hips pushed forward grinding our groins against one another. I ran my fingers through his thick, sandy hair and tugged at it gently. He moved his hand to my belt and expertly unfastened it, then opened my jeans. Unzipping my fly, he slipped his hand inside and rubbed my cock through my underwear. I leant back with my shoulders and pulled his T-shirt free from his jeans and up to his shoulders, revealing a slim, smooth torso. I heard him gasp as I bent forward and wrapped my mouth around one pert nipple.

He slid his other hand into my trousers and with one swift movement pushed both them and my underwear down to my thighs. I moved my mouth to his other nipple as he caressed my buttocks, his strong fingers kneading my flesh. He moved his hands to my head and pulled it up to make me kiss him again. When he broke the kiss he spoke, but I didn't catch exactly what he said. Whether it was the noise in the cage or his accent (I think it was vaguely Scottish) I couldn't tell whether he said 'Do you want me to give you a blow-job?' or 'Do you want to give me a blow-job?'. I decided to take the safe option and smiled at him as I undid his jeans. I pulled them down to his thighs and bent forward to swallow his cock.

His cock was long, thin and uncut. I guessed he'd been out all night because it tasted a bit salty under the foreskin, so I pulled back a bit. I surreptitiously spat on his cock and rubbed it around with my hand to try and clean it up just in case. He reached down for mine and we stood wanking each other off for a few moments. Then I bent forward again and closed my lips around the head of his cock. I pushed my tongue inside his foreskin and ran it around against his gland. He put his hands on my head and pushed me slowly toward him so that his shaft slid effortlessly down my throat until my nose was pressed into his hairless groin. I worked my throat muscles and pushed my tongue against his shaft, squeezing it in my warm damp hole. He groaned again.

I felt his hands slide down my back until they reached my buttocks once more. There he squeezed and kneaded my flesh as I began to slide my mouth up and down his cock in an easy rhythm. Then I noticed movement at the edge of my vision. When I glanced to the side there was another guy stood leaning against the wall, looking down at me while he had his cock in his hand slowly wanking himself off. I was slightly deterred by this until I felt my partner push his hips forward and thrust his cock back into my throat to resume the rhythm. It wasn't long before I noticed movement on my other side. I looked and there was another guy there wanking off as well while he watched our action. I was starting to feel rather exposed as we were near the cage entrance where it is quite light. And after all my trousers were round my thighs with my hairy arse sticking up in the air for all the world to see. It wasn't only them seeing that worried me. I just hoped the watchers didn't get any ideas about doing anything else. I tried to pull back to suggest we moved somewhere more private, but he was having none of it. He moved his hands back to my head and held it in place while he rocked his hips to fuck my face. It's not that I didn't enjoy it. I just felt a bit uncomfortable with the audience that was gathering. Anyone would think they'd never seen two young attractive people having sex before. Anyway, I soon got back into my stride, alternately sucking and licking at his hard cock as it slid in and out of my mouth and throat. It wasn't long before his breath became laboured and his thrusts became faster. Before I knew it he pushed in one last time and held my head in place while he shot his load straight down my throat. I remembered reading somewhere that the stomach juices were powerful enough to kill off most viruses and hoped it was true as I swallowed for all I was worth.

Once he'd finished he let go of my head and I stood up. We still had an audience as he started to adjust his clothes, putting his cock back in his jeans. 'If we'd known we were going to get that much attention we could have brought chairs and sold tickets. We'd have made a fortune,' I joked, but he didn't seem to appreciate it. I followed his lead and pulled my own trousers up and began to fasten them. 'I'm Steven,' I said, 'What's your name?' He just looked at me in disbelief and walked away and out of the cage. I guess getting friendly with your shag was taboo down there. Embarrassed, I finished dressing myself and went home.

Now, it's not that I was just feeling a bit used by the guy who fucked my face or rejected by the guy who fucked someone else. But I don't think it was a coincidence that a few days later I developed a sore throat and my gums started to bleed. Maybe I'm a bit of a hypochondriac, but I think anyone who gets their kicks having casual sex at a cruising ground should make sure they have regular check ups at a friendly GUM clinic. Even though I work at a hospital I still prefer to go somewhere with a bit more anonymity. It's less embarrassing.

Chapter Eleven

TIM

The walk back home was certainly quicker than the journey the other way. Not only was I so annoyed I was walking faster, this time I knew where I was going and followed a more direct route. It felt like I'd been out for ages, but the sun still hadn't risen and there was still a chill in the night air. I couldn't wait to get home and have a long hot shower to warm me up and wash away the filth that remained of the encounter with Colin. To think he always pretended to be such a nice person. That's what made it all so much worse. He was no better than anyone else. All gay men are bastards and not to be trusted. At least I knew where I stood with Pete. He might be inconsiderate at times and spend too much time at work, but he's always there for me in the end.

By the time I reached the house I was also looking forward to seeing Pete. I was a little worried about the reception I would get after my little tantrum, but, if things went as usual, Pete wouldn't have let it faze him. He very rarely seems to get rattled. One advantage of not being overactive in the emotions department I suppose. Although sometimes it would be nice to have a blazing row and clear the air. The house was in darkness. He must still be asleep. I reached into my pockets and realised that I hadn't picked up my own keys when I left. Another foolish result of my leaving in such a temper. I really must make an effort to keep my emotions in check in future. Especially if we were going to make another go of things. Anyway, I had no choice other than to wake Pete up to let me in, so I leant on the doorbell.

There was no reply. I rang again. Still nothing. Pete's not normally a heavy sleeper, he even complains that my snoring keeps him awake, so I was starting to worry. Had he taken something to help him sleep? Had I upset him that much? Then I realised his car wasn't in the drive. He'd probably gone out looking for me. Why had I stayed out so long? If anything had happened to him it would be my fault. He'd had such a long day he might have fallen asleep at the wheel. And there are so many drunk drivers around at this time of night going home after a night on the town. I tried to resist the urge to panic as I sat on the doorstep and prepared to wait for his return.

I really regretted not picking up my watch before I left. I had no idea how long I sat there waiting. It could have been minutes or hours. All I knew was that I was getting colder and I had to get inside soon or I'd freeze to death. I considered trying to rouse the neighbours, but decided that would be unfair since I was unaware of the time. Also things would be a little difficult to explain. The only option I had open to me was to break in.

I looked around the house, but knew I wouldn't find any conveniently open windows. We weren't that careless. The main thing was that I didn't want to be caught. That would be even more embarrassing than explaining why I was locked out in the first place. In hindsight I should have woken a neighbour. My only excuse is that the cold must have reached my brain and stopped it from functioning properly. Mind you, I still had enough faculties to be able to work out the best way to break into my own home and cause the least disruption.

From the rockery at the front of the house I selected a reasonable sized stone with a pointed edge. I went round the back, staying close to the walls to avoid setting off the motion sensitive lights until the last minute. I smashed a small pane of glass in the back door, cleared the loose shards from the hole and reached through. I knew we kept the key in this lock when we were at home to aid a speedy exit in case of fire. I was banking on Pete not thinking to remove it before leaving to look for me. I was in luck. Having to work blind with my arm through the broken window made things rather difficult. And I had to stretch to reach the key. But I eventually managed to turn it and release the lock. I counted to ten while winding my system up like a sprinter on the starting blocks. Then I threw the door open and dived into the kitchen, heading straight for the pantry door. As soon as the back door had opened there was a noise akin to the wailing of all the demons in Hell. I yanked the pantry door open and punched the code into the alarm system and silence ensued. I took a moment to catch my breath before closing the back door. With luck the alarm had not run for long enough to worry the neighbours. They all knew it was on such a short timer that Pete and I often set it off by accident when we arrived home, especially after a night out on the town.

As I closed the door I realised that the wind was howling through the missing pane and it wasn't particularly secure. In the tool cupboard I found a piece of board that would do to cover the hole and hunted for the hammer and some tacks. Once that was secure I put the hammer back in its place (I've been called obsessive about neatness, but it really does make life easier in the long term) and got the dustpan and brush from under the sink. I wrapped the shards of glass in some old newspaper (we wouldn't want any accidents, now would we?) and dropped the whole parcel into the swing bin. Having tidied up after myself, I decided I needed a drink.

In the lounge I looked around to see if Pete had thought to leave a note in case I got back before him. It was unlikely, I know. I had often wondered how such a successful businessman could be so disorganised. Perhaps he's used to having other people take care of the little things for him. As expected there was no note, but the answering machine was flashing to say it had a message. I doubted that he had used its memo facility, but he might have phoned to let me know where he was. The message was in fact blank. I really hate it when people do that. If someone has gone to the trouble of ringing the least they could do is leave a message to say who it is and whether or not to call back. I mean, what if the machine was on the blink? Someone could have tried to leave an important message and it could have been wiped. I agree it's more likely that they just didn't bother, but you never know. It could have been the hospital if Pete had been in an accident. Or would they get the police to deal with that in person instead?

I definitely needed that drink. I went to the cabinet and picked up a bottle. As I was unscrewing it I realised I could use the call-back facility to find out who had left the blank message. I returned the bottle to its place and went back to the phone. I eagerly punched in the appropriate number and waited. At least the caller hadn't withheld their number. My heart sank as I listened to each digit. I couldn't believe it was him. Colin. What did he want? Knowing him, he'd claim he just wanted to see if I got home okay. Just an excuse to try to wheedle his way back onto my good side. Although he probably still didn't realise what he'd done wrong. All gay men are insensitive bastards when their dicks take charge. I shivered and felt dirty all over again after our encounter, so I decided to let the drink wait and head straight for the shower instead.

I left my trainers in the hall, returned the old jacket to the wardrobe in the spare bedroom (that could go to charity the next time I had a clear out) and dropped my jogging bottoms into the laundry hamper. Now naked, I strolled into the bathroom, took the biggest, softest towel I could find from the airing cupboard and stepped into the showerstall. We'd had an extra large unit fitted for the occasions when we felt like sharing so at least I didn't have to contend with feeling cramped. Since I'd been working out for so long I was almost too wide for standard sizes anyway. Closing the cubicle door I switched the water onto hot and stepped into the almost scalding spray.

For some time I just stood motionless letting the steady stream of water draw the pressures of the last twenty-four hours out of my system. Just then nothing mattered at all: Pete missing our anniversary; the wasted dinner; Pete molesting me in recompense; Colin's betrayal of my trust; my trying to sexually abuse him in return; breaking into my own home – I merely let the hot water drum onto my scalp and flow uninterrupted along the whole length of my body. Keeping my eyes closed, I reached for the shower gel. It wasn't where it should be kept. I had to step out of the water and clear my eyes before I could find it hooked on the back of the shower system. Pete must have been the last one to use it. He just never put anything away. Inconsiderate bastard. Feeling the tension starting to come back, I stepped back into the water.

I squeezed some gel onto my hand and then rubbed it into my hair. I kept my hair cropped short, but I found my scalp always responded well to a good, strong massage. I rubbed firmly all over my skull pressing with the tips of my fingers in a tight circular motion. I could feel slight sensual shocks shooting through my nervous system. I leant back and let the water rinse the lather from my head. The heat of the water had now sensitised my entire body. As it flowed over my skin its caress almost felt like another pair of hands stroking me lovingly. With more gel on my hands I started to knead my pecs, nicely rounded after all the work I'd put into them. As I rubbed, my fingers caught a nipple and my whole network of erogenous zones jumped to attention. My nipple was still tender from Colin's teeth. It felt wonderful just to touch it lightly. For all his faults Colin always knew how to turn me on. And he knew how to use his mouth to perfection. I remember once telling him that I'd give him references for his expertise at oral sex. If more people encountered his supple tongue he'd never have trouble finding a sex partner again.

The fingers in the water became tongues. Lapping all over my skin. I leant my head to one side, allowing the water to flow into my ear. The sensation was akin to that when your ear is sucked whole into someone's mouth. Their pulsing breath crashing against your eardrum. I used the tips of my fingers to simulate a mouth: pinching against flesh as lips would fasten to allow suction. This hot mouth found the nerves at the base of my neck and worked them mercilessly. I gasped, which allowed water to cascade over the side of my face and fill my mouth before flooding over my chin and down my throat. I clenched my throat muscles to form a dam and stop myself drowning or choking. I held out as long as I could before I instinctively shook my head and coughed the fluid free.

The hand/mouth moved from my neck over my shoulder and came to rest in my armpit. There it worked over the skin through the dark hair. Straight fingers becoming a tongue lapping along the surface. Finished there, it nibbled its way across my chest, teasing as it searched for my already tender nipple. It found it and stopped, the very tip of the finger/tongue resting on the edge of the aroused stud. Now my entire body had become one massive erogenous zone. The water flowing over me became an orgy of hands and tongues caressing and stroking with only one purpose: pleasuring me.

While my nipple continued to be teased another mouth (my other hand) worked its way down my side nipping at the flesh as it travelled. At my waist it moved across to the hard surface of my abdomen. There it traced the paths between the ridges of my clenched stomach until it hit the sensitive patch between my groin and the top of my thigh. There it lapped at the skin with long sensuous strokes. The tongue at my nipple became more proactive. First it circled the very edge slowly and tantalisingly. Then it flicked at the stud itself, causing a sensation of pure ecstasy. The mouth at my groin decided to compete. It moved across to my balls, massaging first one, then the other before clamping around both of them at the base of my erect cock. My nipple became caught in a loving vice of its own and I turned so that the water beat down directly onto the head of my straining cock. This third mouth was applying pressure to the slit in my cockhead, trying to push the tongue in there and search the insides of my shaft as it deep throated the rest.

I felt the pressure growing inside my whole body. My nipple was crying out as it was stretched to its very limit of endurance, my balls were churning, squashed hard against the taught skin of my stretched sac, my cockslit was desperately stretching to accommodate the prying water. My pulse pounded in my temples. I held my breath. My cock throbbed fit to explode. I could hold back no longer. I threw my head back, my spine arched, my heels left the floor and I cried out a harsh guttural yell as my ejaculation began. Semen pumped out of my organ with such force that it pushed through the water and sprayed the side of the stall. Again and again it pumped, my hips thrusting in time with each spurt until it was finally over. My body sagged, totally drained of energy, and I reached forward to lean against the wall while I recovered.

As I leant there panting to catch my breath after such a powerful orgasm, the water continued to flow down my back. It formed a river between my shoulder blades and followed the channel along my spine and through the valley between the cheeks of my arse. As it reached my anus it was one last tongue gently licking the tight hole. A soothing sensation helping me to come back down gently from the heights of euphoria. As I was determined to stay with Pete, perhaps it was time to let him have access to my arse. I knew he wanted to fuck me, but I'm not into that. Maybe as a symbolic gesture, though. A gift to cement the stability of the new relationship.

There would be plenty of time to think about that later. Now that I had got all the frustrations totally out of my system I could get back to the business at hand. Yes, I had recovered. I reached for the gel and finished washing, methodically taking care to clean everywhere but avoid the overly erogenous areas. I switched the water off and stepped out straight into the plush confines of the towel. I paused only briefly to savour the sensation of the gentle cotton strands before getting down to the task of drying myself. That done, I put the towel in the bathroom hamper and rinsed down the shower stall, taking care to remove all the semen from the walls. The cleaning implements went back in the cupboard; I slipped into a bathrobe which was hanging on the back of the bathroom door and turned the light out as I left.

I was heading back to the lounge for that drink I'd promised myself when I remembered the state of the kitchen. I still hadn't washed the pots from the aborted anniversary dinner. I had nothing better to do while I waited for Pete to return so I decided to finish clearing up. After all he couldn't take much longer to give up the search and come home, could he?

Chores finished, I finally made it to the lounge, selected

some soothing music, poured my drink and continued to relax. I don't drink alcohol very often, but I have a soft spot for a certain brand of very strong cider which has a very profound effect on me very quickly. It wasn't long before the actions of the evening, the soft music, the warmth of the alcohol and the comfort of the reclining armchair took their toll on my system. I dozed off.

I woke with a start to the sound of a car door slamming in the drive. I started to come to my senses as I heard the front door open and close reasonably quietly. At least he was trying to be quiet in case I was in bed. I rose to my feet rather unsteadily. The alcohol still saturated my system and I wasn't quite firing on all cylinders, but as usual my emotions were raring to go. Pete must have seen the light through the lounge doorway and looked cautiously into the room. All differences were forgotten in the relief I felt to see that he was here and safe and sound. I beamed my most welcoming grin and crossed the room to embrace him in a bone-crushing hug. I was so carried away I even lifted him off his feet and swung him around with my head leaning against his shoulder. Before I could get too dizzy I put him down and moved my head to seek out his mouth. I continued my greeting with the most passionate kiss I had ever produced. I still hadn't released my grip and his arms were pinned to his sides while he overcame his surprise and returned the kiss. He tasted of coffee and smelt of sweat so I guessed he had visited some all-night cafe to keep himself awake while he looked, panic-stricken, for me. I suddenly felt overwhelmed with emotion for this person who had been out God knows how long driving God knows where searching for someone he cares for, no, *loves*. Someone who had treated him like a worthless piece of shit. I felt the need to make amends.

Through his tracksuit bottoms and my bathrobe I could

feel his erection rubbing against my thigh. I knew what I had to do. I had to please this man, my lover, sexually. I squeezed tighter with my powerful arms and sucked the last of his breath from his mouth. I ran my tongue around the inside of his mouth. Then along the edge of his teeth. His tongue pushed against mine and I gently closed my teeth to clamp it in place. I eased the pressure against his ribs so he could breathe and let my teeth scrape along the surface of his tongue as he retracted it. I looked into his eyes and traced the edge of his lips with the tip of my tongue. His lips parted slightly and I caught them between my teeth squeezing gently. When he pulled them free I flicked my tongue against them. His head pulled back and I leant forward, pressing my lips around his Adam's apple. I felt him squirm as I sucked gently, so I increased the pressure. Then I grazed that too with my teeth. I moved my mouth down and round to the pulse point at the base of his neck. He whimpered slightly as I bit down hard. He'd have quite a mark there to remember this session by for a while.

As he squirmed I felt his hard cock rubbing against my solid thigh. I gave one last squeeze of my teeth before loosing my grip with one arm so that I could grab a fistful of his hair. He was still effectively pinned against me by the other arm as I used his hair to jerk his head to the other side, giving me access to the other side of his neck. Feeling like a horny vampire, I bore down on that with my teeth too. He moaned again. My bathrobe had somehow come open with all his gyrations and I felt something damp ooze against my leg. The patch of precome spread as he wriggled, but he couldn't break free of my hold even if he wanted to. There are some advantages to working out six days a week. All this muscle's not just for show you know. When I take control no-one can resist.

All this action was bringing my cock back to life and I felt it pointing straight out in front of me. I shifted our position, quickly pulling down Pete's tracksuit bottoms and lifting him again so that my cock pushed its way between his legs and under his balls. When I lowered him gently his balls were pushed down on either side of my wide shaft. I flexed my erection and felt it push up against the firm flesh behind his balls. He groaned deep in his throat. I pushed forward with my hips and the head of my cock nudged its way upward through the crack in his arse toward the edge of his anus. He gasped with pleasure and another burst of precome escaped his cock to spread against my stomach.

I pressed hard with my fingers along the length of his spine and continued to thrust. He yelped in pain as my nails gouged scratches down his whole back. My arms around his waist, I lifted him again and pulled him closer to me. His cock was trapped between our stomachs. I could feel it rubbing against my clenched abdominal muscles as I raised and lowered him in long slow movements. I looked into his eyes and smiled before clamping our mouths firmly together again. I continued to raise and lower him all the while our tongues jostled together. He growled when I increased the speed of my movements. I pulled him tighter and moved faster. He was panting and gasping and moaning until with one deep inhalation of breath he went tense in my arms. I stopped moving and held him even tighter as he began to shake and I felt the warm sticky jets of his come spray up between our torsos. I leant back and one jet spurted up into the air between our chests before falling back down to our groins.

I just held him tight while he continued to shake and jerk in the throes of his powerful orgasm. When it finished and he fell limp into my arms I released my hold against his mouth. I continued to hold him in the air and his head came to rest against my shoulder. I moved my arms lower until I grasped his buttocks in my hands. His arms were now free and he wrapped them around my neck where his head lay. Shifting his weight slightly to adjust his balance I started to move forward and carry my lover to bed.

Yes, I still loved him. And now I was even more sure that I could spend the rest of my life with him.

Chapter Twelve

PETE

The journey home proved almost as eventful as the episode I was fleeing from. I found it terribly difficult to concentrate on my driving. After joining the motorway I just kept my foot on the accelerator without thinking until I almost skidded on a bend. I just had not realised the speed I was travelling at. I had to try to calm down. Imagine escaping a dangerous episode only to be involved in a car crash. I switched the stereo on, but the loud racing music only jarred my nerves even more. I settled on silence as I continued the route home.

I could not get my mind off the narrow escape I had made. I was not sure which would have been worse the physical beating which had seemed so likely or the embarrassment which would have followed it. You hear such tales. I would definitely have lost my job if this sort of thing came out. My clients just would not have anything more to do with me. I would lose the house and the car and end up having to live on state benefit. I would not have been able find any other employment. I would have been labelled as a pervert. My reputation would have been in ruins. I would have had to face Tim and explain why I was found battered to a pulp with another man in the toilets of a motorway service station. But then I would not have even been there if he had not thrown one of his usual temper tantrums and stormed out, leaving me hungry for both food and passion. If he had not made such a fuss over our anniversary, I would have had a quick session with Rick at the office to satisfy my lust before coming home to a late dinner and a peaceful evening. Perhaps even fulfilling my duty with Tim as well to keep him happy. Then none of this would have happened. By the time I pulled the car up on the drive I had laid the entire blame for all the evening's mishaps squarely at Tim's feet. Perhaps it was for the best that he had left. Mind you, with the way my luck was running, I half expected him to have returned in my absence. As I got out of the car I could picture him stood waiting behind the front door wearing an apron and brandishing a rolling pin like a character from an old newspaper comic strip. I was starting to recover my sense of humour.

And that is not all I was starting to recover. Now that I was regaining my composure, my libido was reminding me that it had been toyed with all evening. Once inside I planned to settle down in front of the widescreen television with a nice bottle of wine and a raunchy porn video. At least that could not change its mind and run out on me. Or so I thought.

When I opened the front door I did not hear the familiar hum of the alarm. I was pretty certain I had set it when I left even though I had been feeling rather drowsy. There was only one explanation. Tim was back. Sure enough, if I listened carefully I could hear music coming from the lounge. I did not know how he had managed to get in because I was sure he had not taken his keys with him, he had been in such a huff. But that was not important. What was important was that he had single-handedly messed up my plans for the evening yet again. The guy was becoming a royal pain.

I was not certain what kind of reception I could expect. Had he returned to continue the argument? Had he realised how much worse his lifestyle would be without my support and decided to apologise? I could not face either emotional trauma at that time and decided to try sneaking in quietly to get to bed before he realised I was home. No such luck. Before I had managed more than a couple of steps from the door I heard him moving about in the lounge. Since I had known him Tim had not been the most delicate of people, but all the time spent at the gym had pumped his body up so much that he now had great difficulty moving around without sounding like a baby elephant. I figured I had to face him sooner or later so it would be better to get it over with now. Taking a deep breath, I steeled myself and looked into the lounge.

From his general demeanour I guessed that Tim had been drinking. He seemed rather unsteady on his feet and aimed a childish lop-sided grin in my general direction before bearing down on me. Before I could react I found myself caught in the most uncomfortably tight embrace. I feared that my ribs were going to crack under the pressure of all that muscle. All that muscle that had lifted me off my feet so effortlessly and now swung me around while I was totally defenceless. All that muscle. I could feel my cock growing into yet another erection despite all the disappointments it had faced so far this evening. Perhaps this time it would get satisfaction. With Tim in this drunken state it might even get to savour the delights of that muscular arse. He had been keeping that from me for too long. And after the trouble he had caused this evening I figured he owed me big time.

I was roused from my fantasies as he planted a slobbering kiss on my mouth, covering it with saliva and filling my face with alcohol fumes. He did not seem to notice me flinch and his grip did not ease at all, so I was stuck at his mercy for the duration. Again the thought aroused me and I decided to make the most of a bad job. I kissed him back. Suddenly he squeezed even tighter and I felt the air rush from my lungs. My tongue pushed forward reflexively and he clamped it between his teeth. Try as I might I could not catch my breath. My lungs were starting to burn and I felt I was going to pass out when he finally eased his hold a little and I pulled my tongue back as I gulped for air.

He reached forward as if to kiss me again and tried to catch my lips in his teeth. I pulled my head back trying to stay clear of that danger. Too late, I realised I had left my throat exposed. His lips clamped firmly around my Adam's apple and I felt uncomfortable pressure. When his teeth came into play I panicked and tried to wriggle free of his grasp. He held me firm as he moved his mouth round to my neck and sank his teeth firmly into my flesh. I cried out in pain and indignation. How dare he leave a mark? But my raging erection betrayed my true feelings. There was something exciting about being totally at the mercy of this powerful man. I closed my eyes and gave my body over to him totally.

I felt his grip change, although it did not weaken. Then suddenly my hair was being pulled painfully to move my head to the other side. Having achieved that, he clamped his teeth on the newly exposed flesh. I writhed in response to the sensations coursing through my body and felt the first jet of precome shoot from my cock. God, it felt horny. I was not just dribbling the occasional droplet, but producing so much of the stuff that it soaked right through my jogging bottoms to his massive thigh.

Then he adjusted my position, at the same time yanking the tracksuit bottoms down to my knees. I am no lightweight, but it took no effort at all on his part to lift me higher and then lower me until I could feel his iron-hard cock crushing my balls against my groin. His loosely-tied bathrobe fell open, letting my erection rub against his firm stomach. He flexed his best muscle (at least as far as I was concerned) and the head of his huge cock just touched against the edge of my anus. I felt a twinge as it dilated, betraying my desire to feel his entire shaft up my chute. There was no way he could enter me from that position, but just feeling his cock rubbing against the edge of my hole had me shooting more precome like there was no tomorrow. He ran his strong fingers down my spine and even the pain of the resultant scratches was a turn-on as his cock continued to batter against my tender groin. I felt my hole flex and widen, desperate to be filled.

Then he shifted position again, lifting me higher so I could barely feel his mighty member against my longing hole. He held me tighter so that my throbbing cock was trapped between our heaving bodies. Every movement increased the friction and sent thrills of ecstasy shooting through my cock. He began to lift and lower me, rubbing my sensitive cock against the ridges and mounds of his tensed abdomen. I tried to tell him that I was about to come and it was too soon, but he just clamped my mouth in his again and I could not make any further protests.

He held me tighter and moved me faster. My cock was threatening to explode with the pressure, but could not expand any further trapped between the hard flesh of our bodies. My balls started to churn. I held my breath and pushed with all my might against his powerful arms. The tension built until my entire body was shaking. I couldn't hold out any longer. The whole day had been building up to this. This time there was nothing that could stop it. Every muscle in my body transferred its energy to my balls as they responded with the first massive shot of my ejaculation. All the sperm that had been building up throughout all the aborted attempts of the

131

evening fought to escape at the same time. It flowed almost as freely as urine. It just pumped and pumped and I thought it would never stop.

Even after the semen finally stopped flowing, my body still jerked with the after-shocks of the mighty orgasm. Eventually I collapsed, totally spent, into his arms. I felt on the verge of passing out from exhaustion. I could not tell what happened next, but I knew one thing. It was truly a powerful orgasm, but it was not enough. I had enjoyed it, but it seemed rushed somehow. I'd had my taste of excitement this evening, and all things considered I liked it. I did not need Tim and his volcanic emotions. I needed the varieties of sex and all the thrills and the risks that went along with it. Stuff the stable relationship. I would find some way to make things up with Rick next week and then find out where the best cruising grounds and cottages were.

Chapter Thirteen

THE KID

It wasn't meant to be like that. Maybe I shouldn't have said it, but I just couldn't help myself. Anyway it was true, and it still shouldn't have made him treat me like that. None of them treat me properly. They just don't take me seriously. They don't even call me by my name. I'm just 'the Kid'. It's not as if I'm that much younger than most of them anyway. It's not my fault that I look it. I don't know why I hang round with them either. I guess it was only so I could be near him. Carl. I'd worshipped him ever since I really was a kid. He lived near me and I used to want to be just like him. I used to read about his successes in weightlifting contests. I've still got cuttings of all the articles the local paper did on him in a scrapbook at home. Home. I can't go back there now either. They threw me out when I started hanging round with the gang. The gang that Carl joined, and eventually took over, after the back injury stopped him lifting competition weights any more. I don't know what I'm going to do now.

It was a Friday night and we'd been having a good time in the club. The others were all drunk as usual, but I manage to look as if I'm keeping up with their drinking while sticking to low alcohol drinks so I'm okay to drive the bike. It's not that hard as they usually make me go for the drinks anyway. Once they've had a few they wouldn't even notice if I was drinking mineral water. Anyway, there hadn't been any trouble that night and the gang was feeling restless. I think it was Carl, as leader, who suggested going in for a spot of poof bashing. I really hate that. Not because the poofs don't deserve bashing, but I always have to act as bait. Just because they say I look young and cute. I hate being called cute. I want to be rugged and masculine like them, but I can't help the way I look. I even stopped shaving once, but I couldn't even grow decent stubble. It was all patchy, and ginger in places.

But what worried me most about being used as bait was why I was so successful at it. What made them respond to me? Was it some hidden characteristic that we shared? Did I have the gay gene and not know it yet? Sometimes I even found myself getting turned on to the attention they paid me. But anyone would, it doesn't make me like they are. I hate them for making me feel like that. They shouldn't be allowed to go around seducing people. They deserve what they get.

That night we went to our usual poof-bashing ground at the motorway service station. That meant another job for me. Why we couldn't just ride around until we found a couple at it somewhere or pick on a passing rent boy I'll never know. This way I had to follow some guy into the toilets and let him come on to me. It didn't normally take long either. Then I'd persuade him to take me to a secluded spot in the nearby woods and play along with him until the others arrived. I really hated that part. Sometimes the guys didn't arrive for ages and the poof would be all over me trying to get me to kiss him and let him feel my cock. I'm sure the guys did it on purpose. I wouldn't be surprised if they were really hiding in the bushes watching and getting a real jolly out of it all. Watching me squirm. When they decide the time's right they disturb us and we give the poof a good kicking. Sometimes the poof tries to protest. Then Carl tells them I'm his kid brother and he's there to protect me. I like the feeling of that. Even if he does lie to them about my age. It feels good to think he's there to protect me. That he cares, too.

So that time we sat in our usual place in the corner where people wouldn't pay us too much attention and we had a few laughs over a couple of drinks. Then the first guy arrived. He was distinguished-looking in his designer track suit and looked so well off we could have probably just mugged him, but Carl wanted the fun of the game. He found a table and sat there for ages playing with his food and sipping at his coffee. He obviously had a lot on his mind. The way he was eyeing everyone up as they arrived made it obvious to us that he was a prospective target, but he didn't seem to be too keen to do anything. It doesn't normally take the poofs that long to head for the toilets and an illicit meeting.

After a while Carl decided the guy might need some encouragement. He suggested that I get some more drinks and see if I could let the guy think I was interested when I passed him. Why did he think I should be able to give another guy that impression? Still, I didn't want to let Carl down. I stood up and was about to give it a try when Carl grabbed my wrist. When I looked at him to find out what was going on I saw him staring at something. Another guy had made a noisy entrance, but I didn't see what that had to do with us. That was until I noticed the posh guy staring at the newcomer. So that's how you let someone know you're interested.

The new guy had a totally different look to the posh one. I guess he was less of a businessman and more of a rough trade type. He was wearing jeans, T-shirt and a leather jacket. He'd

obviously noticed the posh guy's interest because he really
played up to him. He sat at the table in front of him and made
a big show of taking off his jacket and stretching to show off
his body. He had a good body too. Nowhere near as big as
Carl, but he obviously kept himself in good shape. More than
most of the others in the gang. They nearly all had beer-guts.
Anyway, it wasn't long before the leather guy got up and went
to the toilets. He gave the posh guy a meaningful look on the
way so he was obviously meant to follow. He took his time
though, as if he wasn't sure about something. Carl let go of my
wrist and told me to follow the leather guy into the toilets as
he thought he was on the game.

I arrived in the toilets just in time to see the leather guy
disappear into a cubicle. He'd left the door open, but I didn't
want to play my hand just yet. I went into the cubicle next to
him and decided to test Carl's theory. I found some paper and
a pen in my pocket and scribbled a quick note asking how
much he charged. Then I slipped it under the wall between the
cubicles. He took it and shortly after it reappeared. Carl was
right about the guy. And he certainly knew how to charge. I
slipped the paper in my pocket and prepared for the next step.
I had intended to leave my cubicle and join him in his long
enough to persuade him to take me to the forest. But when I
opened the door I heard someone else coming into the toilets.
I took my time over washing my hands waiting for him to leave
so I could make my move. Then he came to the sink and I saw
it was the posh guy. So he'd followed the leather guy after all.
Relieved that I wouldn't have to be used as bait this time, I
decided to leave them to it and tell the rest of the gang. Maybe
we could get them both while they were at it.

Back at our table I told the guys what had happened. I
showed Carl the note. I saw his eyes widen at the price as well.
I assured him that the posh one looked interested and we

figured he could afford it, but he did look really nervous so we should give him a bit of time. Carl agreed and we waited. Now that's one thing none of the guys are good at. And they'd got the scent now. They were all eager to progress to the next stage of the game. Still I was surprised when Carl decided we'd go to the toilets and try to get both guys there and then. There were a lot of risks involved with that, but he must have figured it was going to be worth it. He gave Jez lookout duty and made sure the rest of us knew what to do. He'd got it all planned out like a military operation and we've never had trouble with it before, so we set off.

Inside the toilets we took up position around the cubicle the guys were in. I was at the front with Carl. Most of the others were in the cubicles at either side. There was certainly enough noise coming from inside the cubicle. Carl smiled that sweet smile of anticipation he has and casually lobbed his empty drink can over the cubicle door. There was a thud and a shout which suggested we'd got their attention now. Carl gave the signal and we burst into the next stage. Everyone started yelling and shouting like beaters at a grouse shoot. It's the same principle really. All the noise was supposed to scare the guys out of the cubicle into the open where we could persuade them to join us in a trip to the woods.

After a while Carl signalled us to stop and everything was really quiet again. They should have been lulled into a false sense of security and risked coming out of the cubicle into our waiting arms. That didn't work either.

At Carl's signal we moved up to the next stage. We were all shouting again, but this time we hammered on the cubicle door and walls as well. It looked as if the whole thing was on the verge of collapse when Jez dashed in and warned us that someone was coming. The guys in the cubicles slammed and locked the doors, I joined a couple of the others at the sink making like we were washing up after a slash, and Carl stayed by the cubicle door looking as if he was waiting to go in, but really making sure we didn't lose our prey. And it was a good job he did.

While the intruder was using the facilities, one of our intended victims, the posh one, darted out of the cubicle and made a bolt for it. We checked to see if we should stop him, but Carl shook his head. Then he nipped into the cubicle bolting the door behind him to make sure we didn't lose the other one as well.

When the guy finally left, Jez sounded the all clear and all hell broke loose. I didn't know what was going on, but there was a lot of banging about inside the cubicle. Some of the guys were getting irritated at the thought of being left out of the fun, but we couldn't get in because the door was still bolted. If we thought Carl was in any kind of trouble we'd have had no difficulty breaking it down, but he could definitely hold his own against any poof. And he probably wouldn't take too kindly to any of us interrupting him so we just waited for him to unlock the door and let us in.

When he did open the door it wasn't to let us in. He just told us to scarper and headed for the exit. I took a quick look through the open door and all I could see was the leather guy laying on the floor with a pool of blood forming round his head. Then I legged it too.

Disaster struck in the car park. Some idiot had totalled Carl's Harley. All that was left was a tangle of metal in the spot where it used to be. Carl went spare. He was cursing and shouting and kicking at the debris that used to be his pride and joy. I knew better than to try to interrupt him in mid tantrum, but when it started to ease a bit I went up to him and put a hand on his shoulder to calm him down. When it looked as if he'd run out of steam I offered to give him a lift into town. Then he turned on me. I guess he just needed to get some of the frustration out of his system, but you'd have thought I'd made some kind of slur on his masculinity. He's got some sort of aversion to riding pillion so I just said he could drive. It was all the same to me. In fact I'd prefer it that way. Then he had the responsibility for controlling the bike with the extra weight. He eventually relented and we set off.

It really felt strange not being in control of my own bike. And Carl wasn't in any kind of mood to take things easy. He just threw us into the corners without slowing and I was convinced we would come off at any minute. That's why I was holding onto him so tightly. Well, it was at first. It didn't take long before I started to get into the thrills of the ride. I had every confidence in Carl's ability to handle the bike. He'd never let me down before. I somehow felt incredibly safe with my arms wrapped round his massive chest as we sped through the deserted streets. I closed my eyes and pressed my head between his shoulder blades. I could feel the muscles in his back tense and strain as we turned the corners. It all made me feel really secure. My arms were starting to ache with the strain of being round Carl's huge chest so I let them slide down to his narrower waist. Suddenly we skidded off the road and into the trees. I saw a huge oak looming in front of us before I was torn from the bike. Then I heard the crash.

When I looked up Carl was bearing down on me. Then he was in my face. He was shouting and cursing and demanding to know what my game was. Was he blaming me for the skid? I mean it couldn't have been his fault, but I didn't know what I had done. Then he looked down at my groin and I realised what he was complaining about. I had a full erection straining against my jeans. I toyed with the idea of blaming the vibrations of the bike's engine, but I guess I knew that wouldn't have been true. And the look Carl gave me said that he knew it too.

I could feel the tears rolling down my cheeks as I tried to explain things to Carl. The trouble was I didn't really understand it all myself. With a look of utter contempt he turned his back on me and stormed back to the bike. I scrambled after him losing my footing as I went. My legs just wouldn't work properly what with the shock of the skid and all the emotions battling it out inside me. I don't remember what I said. I know I tried to explain that I wasn't like the poofs we beat up on. I didn't want to have sex with every man in sight. That had to mean it was okay. I mean how can it be wrong to feel something special for someone you care for? Carl turned to face me with a look of thunder. And that's when I did it. I couldn't stop myself. I don't know what I was thinking when I said it, but it felt right. As soon as the words left my mouth I knew it was a mistake.

I knew it without having to wait for the look on Carl's face or the slap that sent me reeling to the ground. It might have been a mistake to say it, but I couldn't take it back. And I didn't want to. I looked up at Carl's impressive form and said it again. It was easier the second time. But not for Carl. He slapped me again, then dragged me to my feet by my collar. He shook me and demanded that I tell him I didn't mean it. That it was all some kind of joke. But I couldn't.

With no effort at all Carl lifted me off my feet and slammed me against the tree. I'd seen what he does to poofs and I didn't know if I'd convinced him that I'm not one. He wrapped one huge hand round my throat and I was sure I hadn't. I clawed at his hand with both of mine, but it was no good. He was just too strong. Then he squeezed a little and I was choking for air. I could feel my windpipe giving under the pressure and I was sure I would black out. Then he let go and I slid to the ground, gasping for breath. My throat was on fire and each ragged breath rasped into my aching lungs.

Carl grabbed one of my wrists and held me aloft by it. I was dangling like a rag doll. I hadn't any energy to fight if I wanted to. Then he wrapped a leather strap around the wrist and fastened it tight. When he tied it round my other wrist too, I realised it was my own belt. I didn't know how he'd managed to get it off, but there was something strangely exciting about being bound like that. Before I could investigate the new feelings Carl took hold of me under my arms and lifted me until the belt caught over a low branch. That left me dangling totally helpless.

I tried struggling against the belt, but he'd fastened it too tight and my weight was pulling down on it so that it was cutting into my wrists. I wasn't close enough to the trunk of the tree to use that as support for my feet while I engineered an escape worthy of Houdini, either. I just didn't know what to expect next. Then I felt Carl's powerful hands in the collar of my T-shirt. For a moment I thought he was going to strangle me again, but then I felt the tug as he tore the material along its entire length until it hung loose at my sides. I couldn't understand my feelings. Was this what I really wanted? To be dominated by this truly masculine man? Before I had only felt secure and protected by his machismo. Now I didn't know. I was scared, but excited. Why did I feel like that? Perhaps I deserved what happened next.

I guess I must have heard him remove his belt, but I hadn't realised what it was. Not until I felt it lash along the whole length of my exposed back. I cried out at the unexpected agony it caused. I could feel the heat in the area where the leather had connected. Then he hit me again. And again. And again. Eventually the pain became a dull ache in my back. My throat was hoarse from my agonised screaming. I couldn't tell if the moisture trickling down my spine was sweat or worse. I suddenly flashed on an image of the guy on the floor in the toilets with the pool of blood round his head. Had Carl done that? Is that what he had in store for me?

Then the beating stopped. I was almost senseless by then, just dangling from the tree limb by my belt. When I felt him behind me I was swamped with relief. His strong arms circled my waist and I leant back, eager to feel his protection. For him to make the pain go away. For everything to be all right again. Perhaps I was just being naive.

He undid my trousers and pulled them down to my ankles. I felt the cold air against my back, which was starting to sting again, and my buttocks, which now made me feel even more exposed. I half expected another beating, but couldn't manage to muster enough energy for any kind of struggle. Then his hands were on my hips and lifting me. In my confused state I thought he was finally setting me free. Then I felt something pressing against my arsehole. Before my addled brain realised what was happening, he pushed down on my hips and his cock started to force its way into my arse.

It felt enormous. I was sure my arse was tearing, it was being stretched so wide. I tried to keep him out, but he was pushing down too hard and I didn't have much energy left after the beating anyway. It wasn't long before I could feel his solid abdomen against the cheeks of my arse and his heavy balls against the back of my legs and I realised he was wholly inside me. Now that the pain was starting to ease it was replaced by a strange sensation I had never experienced before. Was this what it was like for poofs to have sex? If I started to enjoy it, did that make me a poof after all?

I felt him pull himself partway out of my arse before thrusting back in again. And then he started a rhythm. Each thrust felt harder and deeper than the last. When he withdrew my arse felt strangely empty as if my guts had been torn out and there was a hollow left behind that needed to be filled. Then he thrust back inside and filled the hole perfectly. At the top of each thrust he seemed to push against something inside me. Something that sent thrills of electricity shooting through my whole body. He just kept pounding against whatever it was and I just couldn't think anymore. The world no longer existed. I wasn't worrying about where I fit into it. I didn't. I was just this overwhelming feeling of pleasure. This ecstasy. I felt my whole body go tense and my balls start to twist. There was one last push against my pleasure centre and my cock took over. I felt my sperm build up through the shaft until it burst forth into the air. Again and again it forced its way out until I was left feeling totally drained.

Carl pulled his cock out of my arse as roughly as he'd first pushed it in. I felt a sharp pain and then just a damp hollow where he used to be. I vaguely felt him tear the rest of my T-shirt from me so I was left hanging there completely naked. And then I heard him leave.

I guess that clinched it. I was a poof all right.

Chapter Fourteen

COLIN

I wasted no time in getting to the hospital. In fact, I'm fairly sure I broke the speed limit a couple of times and jumped at least one set of traffic lights. Fortunately the car park was deserted at this time of day, so I had no trouble finding a space. Not that I'd have worried about something as trivial as a parking fine when this could be an emergency. As it was I ended up parked across two spaces. I found Steven on reception and for some reason he was looking really pleased with himself. I don't know why he wanted to be so mysterious, but he wouldn't tell me anything other than what a great detective he was. He led me through a maze of corridors and ushered me into a side ward, then stood back as if to say 'There you are, get on with it.'

I don't know what he expected from me. I didn't recognise the sole occupant of the room at all. Mind you, it would have been hard to recognise him under all those bandages and plaster casts. All I knew was that it wasn't Tim. I felt my whole body relax with relief. I hadn't realised I was so worried. I think I'd even been holding my breath since we entered the room. Then, just as suddenly, I was floundering in a tidal wave of guilt.

Whoever this was, he was in a bad way, and here I was just pleased to find out it wasn't my ex-lover. That was so selfish. I looked at Steven and he looked perplexed. Then he looked at the poor guy in the bed. He turned to me and said, 'You must know him.' I still looked blank. 'He had one of your calling cards in his jacket pocket.' He indicated the leather jacket hanging behind the door. Now, that looked familiar. I moved closer to the bed and slowly realised who it was. It was Mike, the guy I'd had to ask to leave when I found Tim in the flat earlier that night. The one from the club. I don't know what had happened to him, but he looked in a really bad way. I couldn't help feeling responsible. Perhaps he'd been mugged after leaving my flat. It was a bit of a rough area.

I tried plying Steven for information, but he wasn't much help. All he could tell me was that Mike had been found in the toilets at a motorway service station. In a very pointed way he asked how I knew the guy. He probably hoped for some juicy gossip, but I wasn't in the mood. It was none of his business anyway. I just said he was a friend and left it at that. Looking even more disappointed, Steven finally took me to see the duty sister. She was reluctant to tell me anything when she found out I wasn't a relative, but Steven managed to sweet-talk her into helping. Although nothing was certain until Mike regained consciousness, they felt most of his wounds were superficial. Certainly not life-threatening. There was a lot of bruising, the bones in his forearms had mild fractures, a couple of his ribs were cracked and he had a graze on his scalp. The head wound was the only thing that worried them slightly. The scalp always bleeds profusely even when the wound isn't deep, but there was a chance of concussion. They couldn't test for that properly until he woke up, which they were expecting to be sometime soon. Apparently they were fairly confident that they now had the correct level of insulin for him as his sugar levels had balanced nicely. The nurse must have noticed my confusion as she explained he was diabetic. And that was when she let me know her patience was at an end. She ushered us out of her office, saying she had far too much to do to waste any more time with us.

Back outside Mike's room, Steven tried to persuade me not to get involved. That was him all over. Keep your head down and leave everyone else to their own problems. That's why things didn't work out between us when we had a brief fling a while ago. He kept accusing me of interfering in other people's lives rather than spending time with him. He just couldn't see that sometimes people needed help even if it was just someone to talk to. I just looked through the window in Mike's door and all I could think about was how much he must be suffering in that state. And I still felt responsible. There had to be something I could do to help. Compassionate as ever, Steven tried to persuade me to go out on the town with him. He should have known me better than to think I could even consider having fun while a friend of mine was stuck like this. I'm afraid I was a bit short with him and told him to go, then, and leave me to it. I had decided that I might not be able to do anything about healing Mike to shorten his stay, but I should be able to help make him as comfortable as possible and stop him being too bored. Leaving Steven to sulk, I headed for the little shop by the hospital entrance. It was lucky I never went anywhere without my credit cards.

I scoured the whole shop trying to decide just what to get. The trouble was, I hardly knew Mike so I didn't know what he was into. I had to just work from what I felt would help ease my stay if I was in his position. I started with flowers to brighten up his room. There were some nice mixed bunches which looked really colourful. And they had plenty of greenery with them to help show them off. They also included some buds so the blooms wouldn't all die off at the same time. I also bought a couple of potted plants, thinking they would last even longer. Reading matter was the real problem. I just didn't have a clue about his interests. I went for a wide selection of magazines. One on science-fiction (I'd like that if he didn't), one on sport (he looked quite fit, so he might be sporty and the pictures were good to look at anyway), one on music, (after all he was dancing at the club when I first saw him). I toyed with the idea of the latest gay lifestyle mag, but decided against it on the grounds he might not want to be 'out' while he was here. I got one on cars and the latest in the line of adult comics instead to bolster his macho image.

For such a small shop they had a good choice of fruit. Not just the stand-by grapes, but some of the more exotic varieties as well. I figured I'd play safe and stuck to relatively plain fare: grapes, satsumas, apples, pears and some passionfruit. I was just reaching for the chocolates when I remembered his diabetes. Fortunately they had a range of special chocolates, so I bought plenty of those as I knew chocolate works wonders for me when I'm down. I couldn't think of anything else, so I made my way to the counter to pay. In fact I couldn't carry anything else. As it was, the assistant had to load me up with boxes to fit it all without crushing anything. While I was paying I noticed the music tapes by the counter. Now that gave me another idea. I staggered up to Mike's room and left everything in a stack in the corner, then rushed back to the car.

I rushed home just as quickly as I'd rushed to the hospital. I had to get there and back before he woke up. The car screeched to a halt outside the flat. Again it was only roughly in a parking spot, but I wouldn't be staying long so it didn't matter. In fact I figured I'd be so quick I didn't even bother to lock it. Once through the main door I bolted up the stairs and struggled with my keys in the front door. I dashed to the bathroom, colliding with junk along the way. I really must get the place cleared up. I snatched the personal stereo and speakers from the windowsill and hunted for the headphones to go with it. Back in the hall I rummaged through the drawers of my audio units grabbing as wide a variety of tapes as I could find. There was a compilation of classic dance music, a more recent one, a compilation of popular classical music, a compilation of show tunes, something soothing to help him relax and that reminded me I had some relaxation tapes in case he had trouble sleeping. As I turned to leave the stack of tapes overbalanced and scattered across the floor. Why is it always like that when I'm in a rush? I didn't want Mike to come round until I was back and had everything set up for him. I dashed into the kitchen and grabbed a carrier bag to shove it all in. Finally I was ready, or so I thought.

I was halfway down the stairs before it struck me that the batteries in the stereo might be running low. With my luck they'd run out as soon as he started using it. The carrier crashed against my shin as I spun on my heel. My keys refused to find the lock. God, I was getting so frustrated. Back in the kitchen I dumped the bag and rummaged through the drawers until I found my spare batteries. I threw them into the bag and set off again. It was only when I was in the car racing toward the hospital that I realised I could have just bought some more batteries when I got there. Typical, I always think of the right way after I've already screwed things up. If I'd thought of that sooner I wouldn't be panicking as much. It had taken me far too long. I was sure he'd be awake by now and I wouldn't get the chance to have things looking right for him.

Back at the hospital I left the car, remembering to lock it this time, and ran to the entrance. Then I spotted a florist nearby with some interesting helium-filled balloons floating in the window. They were shaped like comical figures with streamers for arms and legs. The cardboard hands and feet weighed them down so they just bobbed about above the floor rather than floating away. They had one looking like a doctor with a get well message on it. I couldn't resist it so I rushed into the shop and checked out the whole range before settling on that one anyway. Then I looked at the time. Shit, I was sure I'd screwed up this time.

By the time I reached Mike's room I was panting for breath and my heart was pounding. I needn't have worried, though, as he looked as if he hadn't moved at all since I left him. I sat in the chair at the side of his bed and tried to relax a little. If I wasn't careful I'd do myself an injury and end up in the next ward. I decided to start that fitness routine again as soon as I got a chance. Maybe Mike would help me with it when he'd recovered. He certainly looked fit enough. Just then a nurse came in. She was doing the usual checks and wanted to know what I was doing there. I explained and showed her the contents of the boxes I'd left earlier. She thought it was all a wonderful idea and offered to help find vases for the flowers. Between us it didn't take long to have the room looking much brighter. The room was full of colour and the sweet scent of the blooms. The balloon bobbed happily in a corner as if it approved of the whole display. Just then Mike stirred.

We both moved to his bedside, but fortunately I was closer. At first I thought he was having some kind of fit until I realised it was more likely to be a nightmare brought on by whatever had left him in this mess. He was starting to writhe about and I was concerned that he'd do himself more damage so I held his shoulders firmly, trying to keep him still. I was close enough now to hear him murmuring. Nothing that made sense. Something about evil grins and scared rabbits. When it sounded as if he said 'I'm gonna come' I glanced down and saw his erection straining at the sheets and thought it best to do something about it before he got really carried away and embarrassed himself in front of the nurse. I gave his shoulders a slight shake and tried to keep my body between them to stop her overhearing his mumbles.

Slowly he opened one eye and then slammed it shut again. His face screwed up tight and I realised he must be in terrible pain. I stepped back and the nurse came closer to the other side of the bed. She was talking soothingly to him, trying to get some kind of response. Finally he opened his eyes again and looked around. He tried to sit up suddenly but just fell back against his pillows. He looked panicked and the nurse continued to speak calmly to put him at ease. She explained what his situation was as best she could and that a doctor would be along soon to fill in the rest of the details. Then she went to fetch him. Seeing that Mike was still stressed, I moved in again and started making small talk. He just stared at the window in disbelief at his situation. Then he turned to me and asked who I was. It must have been the blow to the head. Perhaps he had amnesia. I introduced myself again and explained how we'd met. He still looked blank and I was starting to get quite concerned. Just then the doctor arrived and asked me to leave so he could examine Mike in private.

I waited just outside the door, watching through the window. It's not that I was being nosy, just that I was anxious and concerned. Anyway, it looked to me as if the examination was getting a little too intimate. The doctor let his hands stray a little too much and linger on Mike's firm body a little too long. And I could tell Mike was flirting with him. And he had that tell-tale bulge under the sheets again. For some reason that started to bother me. I couldn't be getting possessive, I'd only just met the guy, although I do fall quite quickly and get jealous just as fast. No, I think it was just the lack of professionalism on the doctor's part that was upsetting me. He was actually sat on the edge of the bed and they were chatting like old friends. Suddenly Mike looked up and saw me before I had a chance to move. He said something to the doctor, who looked puzzled for a moment. They exchanged a few more words and then the doctor got up with a dark look on his face and stormed towards me. I moved away from the door just as he rushed through it. He grabbed me firmly by the elbow, snarled 'Come with me!' and led me away.

Now I was feeling confused and a little concerned as he fairly dragged me into the duty sister's office and asked her to give us a few moments alone. When she left he prowled over to the door and turned to face me. I couldn't believe what he said next. For some reason he had the idea that I was responsible for Mike's condition and wanted to know if I was there because of a guilty conscience or waiting to finish the job. I didn't know what to say. For a little while I was just stunned that anyone could believe I'm capable of such a thing. And I didn't know what I could say to prove my innocence. I couldn't tell him the whole truth. Some medical staff are still paranoid about treating gay people because of the whole AIDS thing. And besides that, it wasn't my place to 'out' Mike anyway.

I tried to make some excuse about being a friend and how Mike could have been confused as a result of the blow to his head. The doctor wasn't convinced. I didn't blame him. It sounded pretty lame to me too. He even tried threatening me with the police. For a moment I was worried, but then I realised there was no hard evidence against me. I was innocent, after all. I just had to hope that Mike came to his senses before things went that far. Realising he wasn't getting anywhere, the doctor just took my details and told me to leave the hospital or he'd have security throw me out. I didn't know what else I could do so I left the room and went down to the cafeteria.

Some time later I was sat staring into my third beaker of

coffee and still trying to work out my next move. I didn't want to leave Mike like this. I was still worried about him. And now I was worried about myself. I had to try to see him again and sort things out. But I didn't want to risk getting the police involved. Then I saw the doctor walk past the window, get into a car in a reserved spot and drive away. It must have been the end of his shift. Now was my chance. I just had to hope he hadn't considered me so much of a threat that he'd warned the nursing staff to keep me away.

When I got to Mike's room I noticed the blinds had been closed on the window in the door. I didn't know if it was to let him sleep or because he was having some kind of treatment or examination. I hovered at the door for a while, listening carefully, but I couldn't hear any sounds from inside the room. Carefully I eased the door open a little. The room was in total darkness. Mike must have been sleeping. I sneaked in and closed the door just as carefully. Once my eyes had adjusted to the dark I quietly made my way over to the bed. Mike was asleep, but it looked as if he was having another nightmare. His head was jerking from side to side and he was mumbling incoherently. I rested my hand on his thigh, hoping that my presence might reassure him and ease his sleep. He carried on mumbling, but I was sure his eyes were part open so I started to talk to him soothingly. He stopped moving and his eyes snapped fully open. He looked straight at me and I asked if there was anything I could do for him. When he said what sounded like 'give me a wank' I couldn't believe my ears. I glanced down and sure enough, his cock was straining against the bed sheets again. Uncertain, I looked back up at his face, but he was lying back again with his eyes closed in preparation. I looked at his bandages and plaster casts and realised he couldn't do anything for himself, so I decided to give him a helping hand and gently pulled back the sheets.

His cock sprang to attention as soon as it was uncovered. It looked just as appealing as I remembered from last night. I gently placed my hand flat against its base and softly stroked my fingers up towards its head. As I reached the crown his cock twitched and a stream of precome oozed out of its slit. I turned my hand so that only my middle finger was touching his cock. I ran the tip of my finger down along the ridge in the centre of the shaft until it reached the base. His cock jerked up and I slid my hand around it so that my fingers were underneath.

Squeezing gently, I pushed my hand back up toward the head of his cock. I was using just enough pressure to move his loose skin with me and I watched his foreskin gather to cover the crown. When I reached the ridge of his cock head with my fingers another stream of precome oozed out. This time it gathered in the folds of his foreskin. I released the pressure with my hand and the force of his erection pulled his skin taught once more. Strands of precome caught what little light there was in the room as they stretched over the top of his cock. I grasped it round the base with my other hand, keeping it lifted at an angle from his body. This freed my hand at the top of his cock to smear the precome over the head. I rubbed the sticky lubricant between my palm and the sensitive flesh of the head. Then I moved my hand so that only the very tip of my little finger rested against the slit of his cock. I massaged the swollen hole softly and he started to moan. I squeezed the base with my other hand. His cock jerked again and another pearl of fluid oozed out onto my finger.

I grasped the head of his cock once more with a hand now slightly moist with his precome. This provided some lubrication as I slid my hand slowly along his shaft. When it reached the base I slid it back up to the top without pausing. I kept my other hand tight at the base, keeping his skin taught and the sensitive cock head exposed to my touch. I maintained a slow gentle rhythm as I stroked the whole length of his shaft. Mike started to groan.

His precome was starting to get tacky against my hand, so I eased the pressure with which I held the base of his shaft, releasing his skin to slide once more with the movement of my hand. I increased the pace of my strokes slightly and moved my other hand to cup his balls. I squeezed his balls slightly and rolled them around between my fingers. Mike's groans got louder.

I stroked his cock faster and felt it harden in my grasp. I pushed the tips of my other fingers into that erogenous zone beneath the balls where the sack joins the base of the cock: the small, firm mound between the balls and the arsehole. Mike gasped and pushed his hips forward.

I could tell he was getting close and shortened my strokes so that I was rubbing against the edge of the head of his cock. Mike was thrusting with his hips now and his head was thrashing from side to side. When I felt his cock swell until it was hard as iron and his balls start to churn, I jerked my hand as fast as I could and slipped the middle finger of my other hand into his arsehole. With a brief cry his whole body tensed and his hole clamped shut against my finger. I carried on stroking while he strained to contain his orgasm, but not for long. With a sharp exhalation of breath, the first shot of come flew from his cock over his tensed abdomen and splattered just below his bandaged ribs. A moment latter a second shot landed on his rippled stomach. Then a third. And a fourth. I stopped stroking, but he kept shooting. He must have been ready for that.

When he stopped shooting and his whole body went limp, I took the box of tissues from his cabinet and wiped him clean. It took some time because a lot of it had landed in his pubic hair, but he didn't stir at all. Finished, I covered him again, slipped the soiled tissues into my pocket (well, it wouldn't do for them to be found by a cleaner, would it?), made myself comfortable in the chair in the corner and dozed off.

Then I remember having that dream again. The one where I'm running through the forest. I didn't know why I was running. Whether I was trying to escape from someone or something or whether I was chasing after someone or something I couldn't tell. I just knew I had to keep running. The forest was dark and very dense and I kept stumbling over tree roots. I was panting for breath and my legs were turning to rubber, but I knew I couldn't stop or something terrible would happen. The forest was getting denser and branches kept whipping across me. I had to slow to a walk to force my way through the foliage. I was scratched and sore, but I couldn't stop. Then I heard someone cry out and stopped to look for them, but there was nothing there. Literally. I was stood at the edge of a cliff. I swayed precariously and took a half step back to regain my balance. Again I heard the cry for help. It came from beneath me. I looked down at my feet and there was a pair of hands clinging to the edge of the cliff. I looked over the edge and there was Mike hanging on for dear life.

He just looked up at me, those beautiful eyes of his pleading with me to help him. I didn't hesitate for a moment. I just dropped to the ground and lay flat, reaching over the edge to grab his forearms. But it was no good. I wasn't strong enough to pull him to safety. Then he started to pull himself up, slowly climbing up my arms. His fingers were digging into my flesh and I cried out in pain, but I held firm. He was as far as my shoulders now and the weight of his body was pushing my face into the ground. I just stayed as still as I could so that he wouldn't lose his grip. When he grabbed my belt I felt myself start to slip and scrabbled for a handhold myself. Just when I thought we were both lost, Mike reached the top and rolled off me onto solid ground.

Neither of us moved for a few moments. We just lay there panting with exhaustion. Then there was another voice. We both looked up and there was the doctor. Whether he'd been there all the time I don't know. Mike was obviously pleased to see him and he sprang to his feet and ran to where he stood. I heard the doctor say, 'What's going on?' Mike turned and pointed at me, saying 'It was him. He pushed me over in the first place.' Shocked, I started to get to my feet to protest. Then I felt the ground beneath me start to crumble. I called out as I slipped over the edge and scrabbled for a grip in the loose soil. Either they didn't hear me or they didn't care because they just stood there staring at me accusingly as I found myself falling. Falling into a bottomless abyss.

Chapter Fifteen

CARL

I ease up with my grip and drop the blade back into my pocket. I don't want to cut 'im. Least not yet. We're going to have some fun first. 'E decides to try fighting back. I'd hoped 'e would. It's more fun if they struggle a bit. It means you can dish it out more. And 'e looks fit enough to be able to take quite a bit, for a poof.

I let 'im pull free and take a few swings at me. 'E might look fit, but there's nothing 'e can do to hurt me. I pull myself up to my full height and keep my head back so 'e can't reach my face and let 'im land a few blows on my chest. I figure 'e should have realised how useless it is by now so I catch 'is wrists and squeeze. 'E's trying not to show it, but I know 'e's in pain. I can see it in 'is eyes. I can see something else as well and pull 'im off balance before 'e can manage to swing a kick at me. I swing 'im round 'til 'e crashes against the opposite wall and hear the breath rush out of 'im. 'E starts to go limp 'til I'm holding 'im up by the wrists. Then 'e tries to fight back. 'Is knee lands against my leg just missing my balls. So I nut 'im. Then I squeeze harder. This time 'e cries out as I feel the bone giving in my grasp. 'Is knees give way and 'e goes limp again.

I'm not taking any chances this time, and I'm getting ready to 'it 'im with my knee so hard that 'e'll never be able to use his balls again when 'e starts to shake. At first I think 'e's just scared. Then 'e starts to jerk about like 'e's having a fit. I figure 'e's trying it on, hoping I'll let 'im go, but I'm wise to that trick. I let 'im drop to the floor and stand back to watch 'is little act. 'E's thrashing about all over the place. Banging 'imself against the walls of the trap. 'E's good, I'll give 'im that. But I'm still not giving 'im the chance to get away. I don't panic that easy. Not until 'e jerks so hard 'e smashes the back of 'is head against the bog and goes still. I'm still not convinced so I give 'im a couple of hard kicks that'd probably crush a couple of ribs. Then I see the blood running from 'is head and decide it's time we weren't there. I dash out of the trap, signal to the guys and we leg it back to where the bikes are parked.

Then suddenly it gets worse. In the space where I'd left my Harley is a mangled heap of junk. Some bastard's totalled it. And I just know it was the rich poof. I can just imagine 'is face as 'e smashed 'is car over it trying to get revenge. Well, 'e'd better pray I never see 'im again or 'e's dead meat.

When I finally calm down enough to stop kicking at the wreck that's left of my bike, I realise the Kid's there with 'is hand on my shoulder. 'E offers to give me a lift on 'is bike and doesn't even flinch when I turn on 'im. I let 'im know I don't ride pillion for no-one. 'E just shrugs and says I can drive. There's something about the look in those little boy eyes of 'is. A look that's really eager to please. I do need to get home. The others have already legged it. So I give in.

I climb onto 'is bike which is only just big enough for me, fire it up and hold it while 'e clambers on behind me. When we set off it takes a while before I start to wonder about how tight 'e's holding on to me. And I'm sure I can feel 'is head leaning against my back. At first I just figure it's because 'e's not used to riding pillion either and 'e's a bit scared. Then I start to think there's something pressing against my arse. 'Is hands slide lower until they're pressing beneath my waist and the thing poking my rear feels just like a cock with a hard-on. I damn near crashed the bike. I ran us off the road and into a small wood at the side. I managed to keep it under control and we screeched to a halt just before hitting a huge tree.

The Kid had fallen from the bike when we went into the skid and was sprawled on the ground nearby. I stormed over to 'im and demanded to know what the fuck was going on. 'E just looked up at me with fear in 'is eyes and pretended 'e didn't know what I was talking about. I looked down where 'is cock was making a lump in 'is tight jeans and 'e realised 'e couldn't get out of this one. Tears started to pour down 'is face as 'e started to beg. I couldn't believe it. This was the Kid for Christ's sake. 'E was one of the gang. A mate. God, we'd even shared digs when out at rallies. Had 'e been perving over me all the time we'd bunked together? I couldn't 'andle this. I turned and went back to get the bike.

The Kid's on 'is knees crawling after me. Pleading with me. Saying 'e's not like those poofs we beat up on. 'E's not a pervert. 'E don't go chasing after men for sex. It's just me 'e feels this way for. Like that makes it any better. I turn on 'im and 'e's getting to 'is feet. 'E says it's no different to what everyone feels for their mates. It's not dirty like the guys in the toilets. It's not wrong. I glare at 'im, but 'e won't shut up. Then 'e goes too far. 'E says the one thing 'e can't take back.

I can't believe my ears and I slap 'im so hard 'e falls back onto the ground. Wiping the trickle of blood from the side of 'is mouth, 'e says it again! I bend over and slap 'im again. I grab 'im by the collar and lift 'im off the ground. Shaking 'im, I try to make 'im admit that 'e's lying. That it's all a joke. But I can see in 'is eyes it's not. Even worse, I'm starting to get a bit of the rush I feel when I'm beating up on a poof. And I can see the Kid's not lost 'is hard-on despite being slapped around. I figure maybe 'e likes it. So maybe 'e's going to get it.

I lift 'im off the ground and slam 'is back hard against the trunk of the tree. 'E just looks at me real scared. I grab 'is throat in one hand and 'e starts to panic. 'E grabs at my fingers with both 'is hands trying to pull me off, but 'e doesn't stand a chance. I just tighten the grip a little so 'e's choking a bit. With my other hand I reach down and unfasten 'is belt. It's tricky with one hand, but eventually it gives and I pull it free from the loops of 'is jeans. I let go of 'is throat and 'e starts to slide down to the ground until I grab one of 'is wrists and hold 'im up by it. I wrap the belt round 'is wrist and pull it tight so it fixes in a loop. Then I wrap the other end round 'is other wrist and tie it tight. I grab 'im by the arms and lift 'im off the floor until I can hook the belt over a low branch on the tree. It's just high enough so 'is feet can't quite touch the floor. 'E's hanging there like a side of beef. Ready for me to deal with as I will.

I step back for a moment while I decide just what to do next. 'E's struggling at the belt, but I've tied it too tight and 'e's stretched too much to be able to get a good grip on it. I grab hold of the neck of 'is T-shirt with both hands and pull. It tears right down the back and I keep pulling until it hangs loose at 'is sides. 'Is spotty, skinny, pale back's exposed and ready for me. I reach down and undo my own belt. As I pull it through the loops on my jeans I think maybe I can beat some sense into 'im.

I lean my arm back and then swing forward, slashing my belt down the length of 'is back. 'E screams in pain and when I look there's a large red stripe running along 'is spine. Feeling like a pirate in one of those old films punishing a traitor, I start to whip 'is back with my belt. The leather cracks as it hits 'is back and 'e cries out with each stroke. Each stroke leaves its mark on 'is pale back. Then I guess I lost it for a while. I don't know how many times I hit 'im. I wasn't counting. I just kept on and on as if it would make everything all right. As if it would make up for the poof escaping at the bogs. As if it would make up for the other poof hurting 'imself before I'd had the chance to teach 'im a proper lesson. As if it would make up for my bike being trashed. But most of all, as if it would make up for the Kid saying what 'e had.

I don't know how long it carried on for. I just know I didn't stop until I couldn't lift my arm to whip 'im no more. I was panting for breath and covered in sweat. 'Is back was covered in red marks and glistening with sweat too. When I looked closer I realised it wasn't sweat, but blood rolling down where I'd broken the skin with my belt. I started to feel sorry for what I'd done. Maybe 'e didn't deserve to be punished for everything else that had 'appened. 'E was the Kid, after all. We'd been through a lot together. Maybe 'e'd realise where 'e'd gone wrong now. I put my arms round 'is waist to lift 'im down and stopped in disgust. When I touched 'im 'e groaned and tried to push 'imself against me. And even worse, I could feel 'is cock still pushing against 'is jeans. 'E'd loved it and still wanted more! Well, if 'e wanted it, 'e was going to get it.

It was only then I realised that giving 'im the beating had the same effect on me. My cock was rock hard and straining against the front of my jeans. This was what 'e really wanted so I might as well let 'im have it. I undid 'is jeans and pulled them down around 'is ankles. I unbuttoned my fly and pulled my cock out of my jeans. It looked as though 'e liked it rough so I didn't need to worry. I just grabbed 'is waist and lifted 'im up until 'is arse was against the tip of my cock. Then I braced my legs and pushed 'im down so that 'is arsehole stretched over my cock. 'E screamed louder than ever and I felt 'is arse closing around my cock. It felt good so I kept pushing and 'e kept sliding down until 'is arse touched my crutch. I had my whole cock up 'is arse and it felt really good. It was warm and tight and his arse kept rubbing against me as it struggled to push me out.

It all felt so good I just lost it again. I started thrusting with my hips and ramming my cock in and out of 'is tight arse. 'E kept panting and moaning, all the time goading me on. I just kept fucking 'im, thrusting faster and harder and sinking my cock deeper into 'im. I wasn't thinking about anything now. Just focused on giving my cock what it wanted. Suddenly 'e cried out and 'is arse clenched tight against my cock. I made one last hard, deep thrust and found myself shooting my come into 'is guts.

When I'd finished I yanked my cock out of 'im and 'e yelped in pain. I tore 'is T-shirt completely off 'im and used it to wipe myself clean. Then I looked at 'im and wondered what to do next. 'E was the Kid, after all, not just some poof to be beaten up. Didn't 'e deserve better? I don't know what to do so I just leave 'im hanging there and start to walk home.

Chapter Sixteen

MACK

So by the time I finish cleaning up you can guess what kind of mood I'm in. Pity any poor faggot that crosses my path tonight. As I'm locking up I hear this voice calling to me. I turn round and there's Carl crossing the road toward me. Carl's a good bloke. He's one of my regulars that I approve of. Not one of those sissies just trying to look good. He's into serious weights. He's won a few local weightlifting contests as well. He would have gone national, but it turns out he's got a weak back. To look at him you wouldn't think he'd got a weak anything. He's huge. Since he lost his chance with the weights he kind of slipped the rails a bit. He hangs with this local gang, fact is I think he runs it now. And he's been in a few scrapes. He's got the scars to prove it. It takes a brave man or an idiot to cross him and he looks as if someone just has.

He asks why I'm so late and I just say I've been cleaning up someone's mess. I don't go into details in case he gets the wrong idea. Before he gets a chance to ask any more I ask how come he's walking. His face darkens and he says some poof's totalled his bike. Then he gives me the full story about how he'd been teaching these two poofs a lesson when they were having it off in the bogs at the local motorway service station. In the fuss one of them managed to slip away and the other had some kind of fit before Carl managed to deal with him proper. When the gang got outside, Carl's bike was on the floor all buckled. The one who got away must have crashed into it. He says that if he manages to get his hands on any poofs tonight he's going to screw their fucking arses to the floor.

I decide he's maybe fired up enough to go for something special, so I try him out by telling him the full story about how I'd taught Rick a lesson in the tanning room. About how the little queer was putty in my hands and how I'd brutalised his face and his arse. Carl's looking at me a bit funny now so I tell him how it must have hurt the queer 'cause of all the blood he left on my prick. Now he looks as if he can see where I'm coming from and says maybe that's the only way to deal with them. I tell him that, if he's interested, I've heard of this place where queers hang out regularly, looking to be treated rough. Maybe he can get rid of his anger by beating up on some of those. They'll think they're getting what they want and beg for more until they realise they're getting worse than they expected. Slowly a grin forms on his scarred face and he tells me to lead him to it.

Now, the place I was talking about is underground and near some river or canal. It's not used properly anymore and it looks a bit like a building site. It's enclosed and dark and gloomy. One area's caged off and full of rubble and concrete pillars. Maybe all the queers get a rush from how rugged the area is. Anyway they all ponce around in the cage trying to look all hard until they see someone they like and then they can't wait to get on their knees and suck your cock like a baby. It's been a while since I felt the need to go down there, but every time I do I find someone to vent my anger on. It's not like they can report it or anything. How're they going to explain why they were there in the first place? That'd let everyone know they were asking for it.

When we get there I take Carl into the cage and head to the back where all the serious action starts from. Carl's looking really uncomfortable. He's standing real still and not looking around at all. He says he needs to get away from all these faggots shagging or he's going to throw up. I can see his fists bunched up at his sides. I tell him he needs to bide his time, like catching fish, and then when one of them takes the bait we'll do him over good and proper. He just looks at me. Something in that look almost makes me feel sorry for the queer we manage to land. Almost. I show him a small ramp to the side and suggest he waits up there while I find us a victim. He's not keen, but he agrees, telling me to hurry or he'll just tear every one of the fuckers apart with his bare hands. And I think he means it.

As Carl heads toward the ramp, walking rigid as a robot, I move in the opposite direction looking for a likely candidate. When I round a corner I can't believe what I see. There's three guys sucking each other off as if there's no one else around. One guy's sort of lying on his back between the other two, but they're holding him up so he's at the right height. He's got his head back and he's sucking and licking at this other guy's cock and balls so I figure the one in the middle's the queer. Then I see the guy holding him up at the other end is sucking his cock for him. Now I'm confused. They can't all be queer. You either suck cock or you have it sucked. You don't do both, do you? Then it's all sorted. The guy at the end stops sucking the queer's cock and goes in for the kill. He's obviously just been getting him ready to take him by surprise. Anyway he pulls the queer's pants down his legs and, without dropping him, shifts him round so his arse is lined up ready. Then he just swings his hips forward and his cock disappears right up the queer's hole. It looks like the queer in the middle's going to get what's coming to him after all. I reach across and give the guy who's fucking a pat on the arse to show I approve and head off back to the hunt.

It didn't take long before I found the perfect victim. I figured I had to be careful to make sure Carl wouldn't go off the deep end. Anyway, this guy looks sweet enough to be a young girl so I think he's safe. He's slim with long blond hair hanging to his shoulders. He's young and he's pretty so, like I say, I think Carl can convince himself it's a girl so he doesn't worry about being a faggot himself when that pretty face is wrapped round his dick. The blond's just staring at me wide eyed and drooling. I walk over to him, ready to reel him in. When I get there he says something about thinking I was after this other guy stood near him. I hadn't even noticed him before and he wasn't the right type at all, too out of shape. I turn back to the blond and say, 'I wouldn't even touch him with yours,' and he laughs. A girly giggle that makes my toes curl. He wasn't going to be laughing for long. It was all I could do to stop myself slapping him one right there and then.

He doesn't see what's going on and starts fawning all over me. He's rubbing his soft girly hands all over my chest going on about how big and powerful I am. Then he leans forward and tries to kiss me. I nearly deck him, but manage to hold back thinking about how much fun I'll have watching Carl do it later. His hands are all over me still until they reach the bulge at the front of my trousers. When he feels my huge cock he damn near comes on the spot. He squeals about how enormous I am and I just think he's in for a shock when I actually get an erection and shove it inside him. I know it won't take much more before the queer's fully hooked and begging to agree to anything I suggest.

His hands are shaking as he undoes my trousers and forces them down my thighs. My cock flops out and he drops to his knees smothering it in girly kisses. Then he starts licking at it like an ice cream. I figure he'll never get down to some proper action at this rate and Carl's probably getting restless, so I grab the back of his head and shove my cock into his mouth. He's such a wimp he falls back against the wall. I decide it's time to get started properly. I lift him to his feet, pull my trousers back up and lead him to the ramp. I have a quick look round to make sure we aren't followed and push him up the ramp to his fate.

Carl's standing at the top of the ramp, not moving at all. He looks like a huge bomb ready to go off at any moment. When he sees the blond he looks at me, surprised. I realise that in the dark up here the blond looks even more like a girl. The blond stops when he sees Carl and starts to back away a bit. I just push myself into his back so he can feel my powerful chest against his shoulders and my huge cock against his arse. He goes all weak with desire and lets me push him the rest of the way up the ramp. I reassure Carl saying that 'she'll' do for us both before we do for 'her'. The way I stress the 'she' and 'her', he finally twigs. I undo my trousers and drop them to my thighs. Carl follows my lead. The queer drops to his knees and starts sucking on first my cock then Carl's. Carl's cock's big like the rest of him and almost as big as mine while I'm only starting to get aroused. But he's no competition when the queer finally manages to give me a proper erection. I glance up at Carl's face and it's a real picture. He looks as if he's never had a blow-job before. He looks at me as if he's unsure whether he should be enjoying it or not and I just nod a little for reassurance. He closes his eyes and lets the queer get on with it. When the blond tries to move his head away to come back to me, Carl just grabs it with his huge hand and holds it in place. I remember the action I saw earlier and move around a bit so the queer's on the floor between us. Then I move in for the kill.

I bend down and start to undo the queer's trousers. Still sucking at Carl's dick, he struggles to his feet so I can drop them. I shove them down to his ankles and a smooth, hairless hole winks at me. I spit on my hand and work on my cock a little until it's properly hard. From the look on Carl's face I don't think I've time to try stretching the guy's hole. I bet he's had enough people up there to make it loose enough anyway. When I figure my cock's hard enough I line it up and grab hold of his hips. When the tip of my head touches the centre of his hole I can see the thing expand in anticipation and he tries to push back with his arse. I figure he's good and relaxed so it's now or never. I pull back on his hips and push forward with mine to get my cock in as far as I can before his arse clamps down on it. Not bad, I make it about halfway. Most women can't handle that much without loads of coaxing first.

I just know he's screaming with pain, but his throat's plugged with Carl's cock. And from the look on Carl's face he really appreciates the extra sensation he's getting from the blond's cries. Mind, there's only his face showing anything. The rest of him's not moving a muscle. He's just standing there letting the queer do all the work. After a few moments I guess the kid's arse adjusts and he starts going to work on Carl again. Carl still doesn't move and I find I'm fascinated watching the emotion play on his face. Suddenly he plants his mighty paws on the back of the blond's head and his jaw twitches slightly. The queer gags and I realise Carl's shooting his load down his throat. Beyond that he still doesn't move. I can't believe it. I guess he's finished when he moves his hand from the kid's head, but he doesn't pull out. He just lets him carry on sucking. Now I want some more of the action. I push forward with my hips, but the kid clamps down again with a jerk. Suddenly a look of death crosses Carl's face. Without a word he pulls his cock free of the blond's mouth (I can't help noticing it's still erect) and fetches him such a slap across the face he would have gone flying if he weren't still impaled on my cock.

Before the kid has a chance to recover from the shock and register the new pain Carl's grabbed his jaw with one huge hand. He says the little bastard bit him and tells me to stand still. Seeing the look in his eyes even I wouldn't want to cross him so I plant my feet in the ground as he lifts the queer by the throat until he's upright against my chest. I'm sure his feet aren't even touching the ground. Trying to keep my balance, I grab him round the waist. I can see the muscles in Carl's forearm bunch as he slowly pushes down against the kid's collarbone. Carl's strength added to the force of gravity slide the blond slowly down my cock. I can tell he's struggling from the way his arse muscles are fighting against my massive shaft. He's clutching at Carl's wrist, trying to prise his fingers from round his throat, but he doesn't stand a chance. That grip's so tight all the kid can do is gurgle. And all the time Carl's slapping him about with his other hand. Not too hard. Just enough to rock his head back and forth.

His arse is really working on my cock. And watching Carl's massive hand crushing the queer against me while he beats up on him is getting to me in other ways. By the time the blond's arse reaches the base of my cock I realise I'm coming inside him. Not just ordinary coming. It's not shooting out of me, it's flowing like a fucking river. I'm starting to go weak at the knees when I feel the kid going into spasms in my arms. I think maybe he's choking to death. Then Carl actually snarls and with hardly any effort at all pulls the kid off my cock and, still with one hand, hurls him against the wall.

I'm too weak from that orgasm to do anything even if I wanted to as I see Carl laying into the limp form. I'm not sure what set him off until he finally stops and turns to me. There are white stains down the front of his clothes. The kid had obviously come as well. He just looks at me and says, 'He wasn't supposed to enjoy it too.'

Chapter Seventeen

CARL

When I reach town the place is mostly deserted. Well, it is really late so I'm surprised when I see Mack locking up 'is gym. I call out to 'im and cross the road to find out what's going on. 'E just says there's been some sort of mess 'e had to clean up. Then 'e asks why I'm on foot. I tell 'im everything that's happened. Well, almost everything. I tell 'im about the service station and trapping the two poofs in the bogs. I tell 'im how one managed to get away and the other threw a fit and knocked 'imself out before I could sort 'im out. I tell 'im how the first one must have wrecked my bike in the car park and how I'm going to deal with any more poofs I can find. I don't tell 'im about the Kid.

Then Mack tells me what had happened at 'is place. How 'e'd been having trouble with one of the poofs who goes there. How 'e'd decided to teach 'im a lesson by trapping 'im in the tanning room and shagging 'im senseless. The way 'e describes fucking the guy's face and arse it almost sounds as if 'e'd enjoyed it. Now I'm starting to worry a bit. I can't take another mate turning out to be a poof. Is the whole world queer except for me? Then 'e explains how 'e'd really hurt the guy and what a mess 'e'd left 'im in. Getting off on causing the poof pain I can understand. I've been there myself. That's not the worst of it. The cheeky poof actually wanked 'imself off and sprayed come all inside Mack's tanning machine. That's why 'e's 'ere so late. 'E cleaned that lot out, which must have taken ages, and then felt so wound up 'e had to have a full workout to try to get it out of 'is system.

So 'e's got reason to want to do more damage to some poofs as well. And 'e tells me 'e knows somewhere we can do it. Somewhere the poofs all hang out begging to be treated rough. Somewhere no-one will notice when you treat them that bit rougher than they like. It sounds good to me so I agree to go along with 'im.

It's a good job I trust Mack 'cause I wouldn't let anyone else take me where 'e did. I'm getting a bit worried when we go underground and I can hear running water. If 'e does try anything funny 'e's going to end up floating face down in it. The place is really dark and it takes a while for my eyes to adjust. It looks like an old building site. There's rubble everywhere. Mack leads the way into a kind of cage and I follow 'im to the back where it's real dark. The place is really giving me the creeps. 'Specially after what 'appened with the Kid. I've never seen so many poofs in one place. And some of them are actually kissing. Right here where they can be seen. It's disgusting. I tell Mack I can't take much more of this and 'e says it won't be long before we find someone to work on. I'd just as soon kill the lot of 'em right there and then, but 'e says to wait. 'E shows me a ramp where I can go to wait where I won't be looking at all the disgusting poofs and their pervy ways. I tell 'im to hurry up and just manage to get up there without killing anyone.

Mack's right about the ramp. From up there I can't see what's going on anymore. But I can still hear them. The sounds of all those poofs having sex. Sounds like I heard in the bogs at the service station. Sounds like I heard when the Kid was strung up in the tree and had my cock ramming up 'is arse. It feels like I'm left standing there forever trying to block out the sick noises before Mack turns up with a poof to deal with. I can't believe it. At first I think 'e's actually managed to find a girl down 'ere and is suggesting we share 'er. She doesn't look too keen either and Mack almost shoves 'er up the ramp. It's only when they get close that I can see there's a bloke under all that blond hair. I wouldn't be surprised if 'e was even wearing make-up.

Now that we've got the poof away from the others I expect to just lay into the perv, but Mack just drops 'is pants and looks at me to do the same. I don't know what's going on, but I figure Mack knows what 'e's doing. As soon as my jeans reach my knees the poof's on 'is knees with 'is mouth all over Mack's cock. Then 'e turns and starts to lick at mine. Now I'm not sure about this. Leaving my cock that close to a poof's teeth makes me feel kind of at risk. But then I start to have feelings down there I've never 'ad before. I can't describe the way I felt with that tongue licking up and down my cock. When I look down all I can see is a mass of long blond hair falling over slender shoulders and it looks like a girl going down on me. But no-one's ever given me a blow-job like this before. When I feel the mouth stretch around the head of my cock and slide down until it reaches the base I'm in 'eaven. My whole cock is wrapped in somewhere warm and moist and the tongue's still rubbing against the sides of it. A strange thrill shoots up my spine. Then suddenly the sensation ends and I see the poof trying to move away. Well, 'e's not finished yet so I grab hold of the back of 'is head and push it back against my crutch. 'E soon gets the idea and goes back to work.

Now I don't know what Mack's up to down at the other

end, but suddenly the throat goes into overdrive. First my cock's sucked even deeper in, then the sides of the throat keep squeezing it. Maybe it's trying to cry out. I don't know and I don't care. It feels too good. I can tell I'm about to lose it again. Not like when I was fucking the Kid. I'm not getting the animal urges to just fuck 'im senseless. I don't feel I need to do anything except enjoy the sensations in my cock. Sensations which are spreading through my balls and up into the rest of me. I feel my balls tighten and I grab the back of the head at my crutch, keeping it in place while I shoot my second load of the night straight down the 'ungry throat.

When I finish shooting the mouth carries on sucking and the tongue is still licking. I'm still enjoying the new feelings so I just move my hands back to my sides and let them carry on. I'm shocked out of the daze by a sudden stabbing pain in my cock. I don't know what 'appened, but the poof must have caught it with 'is teeth. When I look down 'e's looking up at me with fear and pain and sorrow in his eyes. All I can see is the Kid looking at me with those same eyes when 'e said the unmentionable. And I lose it again.

Grabbing a fistful of that long blond hair, I pull 'is head off my cock and slap 'im with my free hand. I can hear 'is teeth rattle, but 'e don't fall down and I realise it's because 'e's being held up by Mack's cock deep in 'is arsehole. Then I see just how huge Mack's cock is and that 'e's been struggling to get it all inside the poof. I remember how good it felt to have my cock sunk deep in the Kid's arse and decide Mack should have a helping hand. I tell 'im to brace 'imself and 'e does.

I've got the poof by the throat and I push 'im back until 'e's right back against Mack's chest. 'E's struggling like mad with 'is hands against my wrist trying to pull me loose. Then I see my hand round the Kid's throat, 'im struggling to get free while I undo 'is belt. If the Kid couldn't do it this poof certainly can't. I just squeeze a bit tighter until 'e's choking and push down so that 'e takes Mack's cock all the way. Then 'e makes like the Kid again. Looking at me with those eyes. Saying those things in my head. I'm squeezing tighter and slapping 'is face, but I can still hear the Kid's voice in my head.

When I feel the poof stop moving down I realise 'e's reached the base of Mack's cock. And from the look on Mack's face 'e's coming inside 'im. Then I feel something splash against my front. I glance down and the poof's coming all over me. Disgusted, I pull 'im off Mack's cock and sling 'im against the wall. Gasping for breath, 'e's still jerking about with come still squirting from 'is cock. I see the prostitute jerking about on the floor in the bogs and decide I'm not going to be cheated again. I lay into the poof with my fists and my feet and don't stop until I'm fighting for breath.

It's no good. I look down at the battered mess and I still can't get the Kid's voice out of my head. What am I supposed to do now that 'e's told me that? What was 'e thinking to tell me that 'e loves me?

Chapter Eighteen

TERRY

It really was a lousy night. It got off to a bad start when Rick
didn't turn up for our regular workout session. Oh yeah, he
called to let me know he couldn't make it; some excuse about
working late, which probably meant he was shagging the boss
again. But he didn't call me until after I'd got to the gym and
already changed into my workout gear. I was even in the middle
of my warm-up routine when Mack, who owns the gym, came
and told me my gym bag was ringing in the changing room. If
I'd known earlier I wouldn't have gone either, but I'd have felt
a real fool if I just changed back into my clothes and went
home then. It's not that I'm too lazy to work out on my own,
but I don't feel comfortable in that gym without Rick's moral
support. Everyone else is so much bigger than me it gives me
an inferiority complex. And they're all so straight. You know,
real knuckle-scraping hetties. Anyway, I hurried through my
workout, keeping myself focused on what I was doing and trying
to ignore everyone else. A couple of times I was sure I caught
Mack giving me strange looks in the mirror. He really gave me
the creeps. I was so spooked I didn't even stay for a shower
after I finished exercising. I just rushed home to get ready for

a wild night on the town. Some hope of that!

I suppose things weren't too bad at the club. At least not at first. Mind you, I'd had my usual half bottle of wine while I was getting ready so it didn't take me long to get tipsy when I arrived there. The music was quite good. The DJ was working a wonderful mixture of old classic hi-NRG, recent cover versions and modern dance tunes, which made sure the dance floor was always busy. I'd done the circuit of the whole club several times and, although I'd bumped into a few friends, I hadn't found anyone worth making a play for. I suppose to be honest there were a couple of likely prospects, but they all seemed to be already spoken for or just not interested. There's no accounting for taste. I was stood by the dance floor watching the action there when I spotted Mike.

Mike's an escort who I've used in the past. He's not bad, but he definitely has an attitude problem. He was by far the most attractive person in the club that night and he knew it. From the way he was moving on the dance floor I figured he was touting for business. And I didn't think he'd have long to wait if the number of people lined up along the edge of the dance floor drooling over him was anything to go by. But he didn't seem to be trying to catch anyone's attention in particular. In fact he was doing an excellent job of ignoring everyone else and just dancing away on his own. He's quite a mover. He dances with his whole body, unlike most people who either dance from the hip or just shuffle their feet. And the clothes he was wearing were tight enough to give everyone a good view of his athletic body flexing underneath.

When the record stopped so did Mike. He strolled from the dance floor totally oblivious of everyone else and walked straight to the bar. You could see the looks of lust and disappointment on all the faces by the dance floor as he walked past them without even a glance. I'd been there before and at that moment all I really needed was a trip to the loo. So that's where I went.

When I came out of the loos I passed Mike on his way in. I decided to hang around a bit and see if he came out or if he was looking for business in there. He came out too soon to have done anything other than what you normally do in the loo. I caught his sleeve to stop him carrying on past me. He turned and told me he was on a night off. As I said to him, that just meant we could do it without my having to pay. He was considering the prospect when he said he saw a friend and shot off to speak to him.

I followed him through the crowd until he stopped near this really dorky-looking guy. Well, the guy didn't seem to recognise him at first because he looked really surprised, but Mike carried on as if they were long-lost pals. It all looked a bit fishy to me. Perhaps Mike was trying for a punter after all. They moved over to the dance floor and I followed.

They were laughing and dancing together at the side of the dance floor. I still wasn't sure what was going on between them, but Mike was my best prospect for a shag that night and if they were just friends that shouldn't get in my way. I decided to find out. Ignoring the new guy, I asked Mike a few discreet questions. He insisted they were just friends, so it looked like I was in with a chance. I joked about telling Mike's friend about his choice of career to see what sort of reaction I got. I don't know. Maybe I was expecting him to make some kind of choice. The new guy or me. And he did. He rushed onto the dance floor and looked straight at me before starting to dance. I didn't waste any time in following him and falling into step with him.

As I said, Mike's an energetic dancer and it's not easy keeping up with him. He was all over the place, but I managed to stick with him until suddenly the other guy muscled in again. After a little spin Mike found himself jammed up against the guy and he wasn't about to let Mike go in a hurry. Then the music took a slow turn and things got really disgusting. They starting rubbing themselves against each other. It was almost as if they were having sex right there on the dance floor. Some people have no sense of decorum. In fairness, it did look as if Mike tried to get away at one point, but the new guy seemed to pull him closer and kissed him. They were in a world of their own. At least they should have been, so that the rest of us wouldn't have been subjected to that sad spectacle. They were still at it when the music stopped and the lights went up. The guy even had his hand down the back of Mike's pants. Mike at least had the decency to look embarrassed as they left the dance floor and rushed to the cloakroom. I decided there was no point hanging around there anymore, picked up a copy of the free papers, got my coat and headed to my Land Rover to start the journey home.

Well, I had intended to go home. In the car park I bumped into Duncan, a young friend of mine, and we got chatting. He told me about this new sauna that had opened up outside town and we decided to give it a try. The address was in an advert in the free papers and Duncan assured me he knew how to get there. I should have known better than to believe anything he said when he'd been drinking. We drove round for ages and we didn't seem to be any closer to finding the place. I finally gave up when Duncan passed out in the passenger seat. I started following the signs to get back to the motorway into town.

After a while the cold night air started to take effect on the alcohol in my system and my bladder started to let me know it needed to be emptied. Fortunately we weren't too far from a service station. I pulled in without paying too much attention to how I parked – I was getting pretty desperate by now – left Duncan to carry on sleeping and rushed for the loos.

Now, I don't know what was going on, but I could have sworn I heard a racket as I was nearing the gents. It stopped before I reached the door and I was desperate, so I went in anyway. The place was pretty full with people milling about and there was even one guy waiting to use one of the cubicles. I managed to find a vacant urinal and started to relieve myself. Then one of the cubicle doors flew open with a crash and Pete rushed out of it. He looked a bit flustered and just walked straight out without even stopping to wash his hands. Now, from what Tim had told me around that time, the odds were that Pete was up to no good. I even half expected to see someone else follow him out of the cubicle and I doubted that it would be Tim. But the guy who had been waiting just raced in, obviously in a hurry to get down to business. I made a mental note to speak to Tim about it the next day and finished off what I was doing. Being more health conscious, I made sure I washed my hands before going back to the Land Rover.

I climbed into the driving seat, slammed the door, started the engine and slipped the Land Rover into reverse, ready to back out of the parking space. I was still wondering about Pete's mysterious appearance from the toilet cubicle when suddenly a figure loomed out of the darkness of the passenger seat and lunged toward me. At the same time I could hear a loud roaring and see a bright flashing light. I was so startled I lost control of the clutch. The Land Rover jolted backwards before stopping with a loud crash and the squeal of buckling metal.

The interior light came on and I saw Duncan smiling sheepishly at me. I'd forgotten he was there. The noise of the door closing and the engine starting had disturbed his drunken slumber. Forgetting where he was, he'd just known there was another body next to him and reached across to do what came naturally. Now that my heart had stopped trying to force its way out of my mouth, I realised that all the noise and flashing lights had been a car alarm somewhere nearby. I just sat there for a few moments waiting for the last of the adrenaline to work its way out of my system.

Then good old Duncan suggested we go have a look to see what the damage was. Reluctantly, I turned the lights on and climbed outside. Miraculously the Land Rover wasn't badly damaged. The sound of metal buckling had made me think I'd backed into a wall. It hadn't been the Land Rover buckling, though. It was a massive, flash-looking motorbike which now lay in a mangled heap under my back wheels. Duncan just looked appalled and asked what we should do. I thought of the leather-clad gang I'd seen in the loos and decided I didn't want to wait around and exchange insurance details with them. No-one was around so I suggested the only sensible thing to do. We got back in the Land Rover and got out of there as fast as we could, the mangled motorbike giving another groaning cry as we pulled away from it.

As we drove away Duncan told me that he was still feeling horny and suggested we go back to my place. Now Duncan's a sweet guy, but he's just not my type. With his long blond hair and slim build he looks quite feminine and I tend to go for more masculine men. I guess it's just a type thing. On top of that, I wasn't sure he was sober enough to perform anyway. But I was feeling rather horny myself so I suggested we pay a visit to the cruising ground instead. He was definitely up for that.

Now, you can play the cruising ground in one of two ways. You either wander around waiting for someone to arrive who takes your fancy or you just go for whoever's available. The whole atmosphere down there is so heavy that you can get so turned on you'd do it with any old dog just to relieve yourself. If you wander deep enough into the place you can find areas so dark you don't even have to look at whoever it is you're involved with, so you don't know whether they're a dog or not. It's just one way of satisfying the primitive urge without having to invest the time and effort to find someone you fancy who fancies you as well.

I had a quick wander around with Duncan, but no-one really took my fancy. He saw a couple of likely-looking prospects and decided to wait to see if he could attract the attention of either of them. It was already very late so I didn't want to spend the time waiting to see if anyone decent wandered into that part of the grounds. And I don't feel comfortable that far into the caged-off area anyway. It might add to the atmosphere when you're in the mood, but after everything else that had happened that night I just didn't feel safe. I left Duncan leaning provocatively against a wall and wandered back to near the entrance. There I could just latch onto anyone half-decent as soon as they arrived.

It wasn't long before someone wandered past looking as if he was about to leave. He stopped at the entrance when he saw me and turned back. He was nothing special really, a bit older and less well built than I like, but he wasn't a total dog so I figured he'd do. He was obviously interested in me, I could see him assessing my various assets, but he seemed to take forever before he made a move. Even then he just smiled sheepishly and strolled over to lean against the wall near me. I decided I was fed up with waiting so I just moved in front of him, leant forward and planted a deep passionate kiss on his lips.

Now that was about as much effort as I planned to put into this little encounter so I pulled back and waited for him to take the hint. I definitely had him turned on and the next move was his. He lifted me off the ground and twisted me around until my back was to the wall and started to kiss me again.

This could have gone on forever and I wanted to speed things up a bit. While he ran his fingers clumsily through my hair I reached down, unfastened his belt and opened his jeans. I was trying to get into his underwear when he pulled my T-shirt up and started to suck on my nipple. I gasped as the cold air hit my naked chest and tried to move things on by pulling his trousers and underwear down his legs. He just moved across to my other nipple. I couldn't be arsed to wait any longer so I just got hold of his head and pulled it back up to face me intending to give him directions. He just kissed me again. I really needed to get control here so I broke the kiss and asked if he was up for a fuck or only a blow-job. He looked a little uncertain for a moment before pulling my trousers down and bending forward to swallow my cock.

He didn't keep it down there for long before he pulled his head back and started to stroke it with his hand. I don't know whether he was just admiring the shape and size or if he was trying to get me to settle for a hand-job. I reached for his cock and figured that I might spur him on a bit if I played around with it. Sure enough it wasn't long before he had my cock back in his mouth. But he was just farting around shoving his tongue in my foreskin and then licking at my shaft as if we had all the time in the world. I grabbed hold of his head and pulled him forward until my cock slipped down his throat. Now that was better.

Preparing to begin fucking his throat, I looked up and groaned in disbelief. Someone much more attractive had just arrived and walked over to watch our action. It was just my luck. I should have waited a bit longer. I wondered if he would join in if I upped the ante. Maybe I could even ditch the first guy and move on to him instead? I leant forward and started playing with the buttocks of the guy who was clumsily sucking at my cock. Maybe I could get the new guy to fuck him and liven things up a bit. But he seemed content to just play with himself while he watched us at it.

Then the guy at my groin stopped moving so I looked down to see what was going on. He was looking at the new guy and I couldn't quite make out his reaction to the extra presence. I just knew I wasn't prepared to take the chance of him moving on to the new guy and leaving me out in the cold so I started to thrust with my hips and began fucking his face.

Then another guy arrived and stopped at the other side of me and pulled his cock out too. I was just wondering how to turn this into a full-blown orgy when the guy sucking my cock noticed him as well. Now he definitely looked uncomfortable and I think he was about to pull back and give up on sucking my cock. I wasn't about to let him do that. I grabbed the back of his head and carried on thrusting. The other guys were quite happy to just watch and wank themselves off, so I damn well wanted to make sure I got off as well. I kept thrusting into his throat until I could feel the pressure build up in my balls. The guys around us wanked faster as they saw me increase the pace of my thrusts. They were groaning along with me as I felt my sperm climb up my shaft. I tensed up trying to hold it there as long as possible. Then I saw the guy to my right start to shoot. Then the guy to my left and I couldn't hold back any longer. With one final thrust I unloaded my balls straight down his throat.

Drained, I let go of his head and started to adjust my clothes. The other guys put themselves away and started to move off. He made some inane comment about charging the audience while he did himself up. Then he even tried to speak to me. I mean it was only a quick shag. I didn't want to get to know the guy. I just wandered out and left him to it.

I got halfway back to the Land Rover when I remembered

about Duncan. I was very tempted to leave him there, but he'd only have a go at me next time I saw him. And besides, his place was nearer than mine and I might be able to persuade him to cook me breakfast before I went home. I went back into the cage and had a quick look around for him.

When I found him he was in a lot deeper than I was comfortable with. He was at the top of a ramp and involved in a heavy threesome with two huge guys I couldn't see properly. I was about to move closer to the ramp for a better view when the guy at Duncan's head started to slap him about. He grabbed him by the throat and lifted him off his feet. He carried on slapping Duncan as he pushed him further and further down onto the cock of the guy behind him. I knew Duncan was into having it rough so I figured he was enjoying himself and decided to leave him to it. Besides, if he wasn't enjoying it and I interfered, the guys might turn on me next.

I just turned round and went home.

Chapter Nineteen

STEVEN

After the quick shag at the cruising ground there wasn't much time left before the start of my next shift, so I made my way back to the hospital. Sometimes it works out that way. You no sooner finish one shift than you're due to start another. I really find that my system copes better if I don't even try to get any sleep rather than making do with a couple of hours, which is why I tend to go out between shifts like that. I have a bit of fun, maybe manage a quick shag, have a quick shower back at the hospital and slip into the change of clothes I keep in my locker for just such an eventuality. Then I head into the canteen and stoke up on caffeine to keep me awake.

I was in the middle of my caffeine fix when I saw Colin stagger into the canteen. He looked as if he'd been at the hospital all the time since I left him. And it wouldn't surprise me. I just hoped the jerk in the coma appreciated him properly. I called him over and told him all about my exploits at the cruising ground while he ate his sandwich. I didn't go into too much detail, he's a bit prissy that way, but I told him about the gorgeous hunk who wasn't interested, the risky threesome and the handsome Scot who I serviced in the end.

Then he told me what had happened to him. I couldn't believe it. What an ungrateful little shit. I don't care what Colin said, I know that any form of amnesia is very rare. Even though diabetics are prone to lapses in short-term memory, after a hypo they very rarely forget who people are altogether. And there's just no way that anyone who knows Colin could suspect for even one moment that he could do that sort of damage to someone. But I would if I got the chance to have some time alone with Mr Amnesia. I demanded to know which doctor had been involved so that I could patch things up. From Colin's description it had to be Doctor Charles. He's the only staff member with 'jet black hair, deep blue eyes, the body of a model and a bulge to die for'. Actually, I know he's seriously well-hung. I've seen him in the showers.

It also explained a lot. As I told Colin, the guy had been involved in a violent relationship himself. He'd let himself be beaten near to death before he found the strength to get out of it. Now that he's mostly over the trauma he does everything he can to help anyone he thinks may be trapped in a similar situation. And that includes being overly suspicious in cases like this. I offered to sort things out – hey, any excuse to get to spend time with Doctor Charles was fine with me – but Colin said he'd do it himself. I just hoped he wasn't getting smitten by the good doctor as well. I volunteered to see what shift the doctor was working and when he'd be available. I was fairly certain he would be around right then, but I wanted a word with him myself before Colin saw him.

I found the good doctor, as I had expected, in the office going over some case notes before doing his rounds. I knocked on the open door and felt my knees go weak as he looked up at me with those gorgeous sky-blue eyes. When he smiled as well, my legs turned to jelly and I nonchalantly leant against the door frame to keep me from falling literally at his feet. He told me to stop messing about and that he didn't have time to listen to my latest exploits because he was a little behind. I made some inane joke about what a cute behind it was. I know it was bad, but my brain turns to mush whenever he's around. Then I explained that I was there on a mission of mercy. To give him his due he didn't laugh in my face. He just raised an eyebrow and looked rather amused.

He looked less amused when I started to explain about Colin and the guy in the coma. He said he was just about to have a chat with the guy to see what had happened, but if I knew anything about it then I shouldn't keep it to myself. I hurriedly told him that I didn't, but I did know Colin. And I would stake my life on him not being involved. He's the kind that gets filled with remorse for even the slightest thing and can't do anything to hide his guilt. If he was Roman Catholic he'd have to have his own personal priest on call to take all the confessions he'd make. On the other hand, making damn well sure that he was there if he saw even the slightest chance of being some help to someone that he even vaguely knew was right up Colin's street.

The doctor gave me one of his knowing smiles. The ones that say, 'I know there's more to this than you're telling me, but I'm not going to pry because I know you'll tell me eventually.' I managed to fight back the urge to kiss him and explained that Colin was waiting in the canteen and would like to see him to explain for himself. The doctor just said that I'd better hurry up and get him because he couldn't wait to find out more about this paragon of virtue. I hoped the twinkle in his eye didn't mean what I thought it might. He had a wicked sense of humour at times, and I knew Colin had a tendency to take things far too seriously. Anyway, I fetched Colin to the office and left them to it while I got ready to start work.

Back at my desk I couldn't stop thinking about what a little shit the guy in the coma had been. All the trouble he could have caused for Colin. And after Colin had done so much for him. I was determined to do something about it. Perhaps I could arrange for him to have an enema? Or a blanket bath from Helga the Hun, the fifteen-stone nurse on the geriatric ward? Or perhaps I'd even go so far as to get him a visit from that nice little old lady volunteer. She means well, but I was sure she'd drive him crazy. Then I noticed that his file was waiting to be completed. I mean, you can't take details from someone in a coma, can you? Now he had apparently come round it was time to finish the job.

When I got to his cosy little side ward everything was in darkness and he was sleeping like a baby. Well, I could soon stop that. I pulled open the curtain and gave him my most cheerful and loud greeting. He was still struggling to come round properly when I laid in to him with the questions I needed to have answered for his file. He was so dozy I'm sure he would have even told me his cock size if I'd asked. I decided to go for it and asked what had happened the night before. He played dumb and looked so woozy I was half inclined to believed him. But not quite.

I asked him about Colin and he tried to deny getting him involved. I kind of lost my temper a bit then and laid it on a bit thick, saying that Doctor Charles would have called the police and that wouldn't be too good for him, would it. After all, even I could work out that someone being found in that state in a public loo was probably up to something fishy. And it wasn't that much of an exaggeration. The doctor probably would have got the police involved if the guy stuck to his story when they talked later. The guy looked a bit taken aback, but there's no stopping me once I get started. I started to list all the things Colin had done for him while he was asleep. He tried to belittle everything and I was getting more and more wound up. I was even dumping things on top of him from his locker. He's lucky I didn't hit him with the pot plants. When I noticed Colin looking in at us through the window, I suggested to the guy that they have a little talk to each other. The guy was starting to falter in his arguments. Eventually he agreed and I dragged Colin into the room and hurried out before I banged their heads together.

I leant against the corridor wall and took deep breaths to calm me down. Maybe I needed more sleep. Maybe I needed less caffeine. Either way I was totally strung out. Then a voice snapped me out of my little meditation. I opened my eyes and there stood Doctor Charles. He looked a little concerned, so I made some excuse about the strain of working two shifts so close together. He could empathise with that. I asked how things had gone with Colin and he smiled his charming smile. He wouldn't give me any details, he's not that sort of person, but did say that Colin was a decent bloke and he wouldn't mind getting to know him better. This was doing nothing to improve my mood. I'd been working on the good doctor for months now and Colin just breezes in and looks like whisking him away from right under my nose. Then he said he had an invite to dinner at Colin's sometime. That was it. I knew all about Colin's little dinner parties. He doesn't cook unless it's for something really special. And I knew the doctor would be special. And I won't mention the time that Colin came to dinner at my place and had the other guest for dessert.

Now I was fuming. And I think the doctor noticed. He had that wicked grin that suggested he could have been just winding me up, but I wasn't taking any chances. He looked through the window into the room where Colin was deep in conversation with the coma guy. He said he had been going to check on the patient, but didn't want to disturb them so he'd call back later. When he walked off I swear there was a spring in his step and

193

he was singing 'Love is in the air'.

It was time to take drastic action. I slammed the door open and made an entrance that the Wicked Witch of the West would have been proud of. I was thinking on my feet, but I hit the patient with everything I could think of that would make his stay in the hospital sound insufferable. He got the idea and whimpered about wanting to go home without me even having to play my trump card of Helga the Hun and the bed bath. I said he couldn't go home because he needed someone to look after him. I was banking on him being enough of a loner to have no-one waiting at home. He hadn't mentioned anyone when I was taking his details. Sure enough, he was looking incredibly uncomfortable when Colin leapt to his rescue. Good old Colin, predictable as ever. I fought to hide a smug grin and look upset instead, as if that would be the last thing I wanted. Sure enough, the guy took the bait and agreed without hesitation. I made one of my best exits, saying something about having a lot of paperwork to organise for something so irregular.

Once I was sure I was out of their view I punched the air in celebration. I do so love it when everything goes according to plan.

Chapter Twenty

COLIN

I woke with a start to find a nurse looking at me with some concern. It was the one who had helped me with the flowers earlier. She asked if I was okay and I told her it was just a bad dream. She said I'd been spending too much time in the hospital and asked if I'd been there all the while since she left. When I said I had, she told me to take a break because Mike wasn't going anywhere and I'd be in no fit state to help him if I didn't. Reluctantly I agreed. With one last look at Mike sleeping peacefully amid his bandages I left the room and headed for the gents.

As it was a hospital they were used to people spending the night. The gents had all the facilities you would expect to find in a motorway service station, including vending machines with freshen-up kits. I found enough change in my pocket to buy one. I splashed water on my face and that helped me to wake up a bit, but I didn't feel truly human again until I cleaned my teeth. The brush from the vending machine was a bit hard and scratchy. And the toothpaste had a strange aftertaste. But it was better than nothing. Feeling a bit more alive, I decided to go to the canteen. Perhaps something to eat and some coffee would bring me round properly.

My body clock was totally out of sync. After the night at the club, everything that had happened with Tim and the mad dash to get things sorted here, I felt as if I'd hardly slept and it should be breakfast time. When I reached the canteen I discovered it was actually mid to late afternoon and the place was full of staff getting ready to start their shift. My stomach was still expecting breakfast and couldn't deal with anything heavy, so I settled for some sandwiches, a chocolate bar (I needed the energy) and coffee. As I paid I heard someone calling to me. I looked around and saw Steven at a table in the corner. He waved me over to join him.

God, but he looked rough. I wouldn't be surprised if he hadn't had any sleep in the time since his last shift. Thinking about it, it couldn't have been that long since his last shift. I asked him about it and he explained that sometimes the rota works that way. You've hardly left from one shift before you're due back to start the next. That's why he often went out with friends when that happened. He found it easier to just stay up and catch up on his sleep after the second shift than to try sleeping in between.

I listened with only slight surprise when he told me about his escapades since I last saw him a few hours ago. He had always enjoyed playing a little on the wild side. I had heard about the cruising area, but hadn't been down there myself. Okay, I'd been down there, but I hadn't done anything. I'd heard so much about it that I was curious to know what it was really like so I went down with Steven once. I didn't like it at all. It was dark, it was grimy and it smelt revolting. The whole thing scared me. I mean, people were casually getting off with each other with no thought to the risks. You could get mugged or worse while you were down there. Steven had managed to persuade me to go into the cage with him, just for the experience, but I stuck to him like glue. I was careful not to even look at anyone else in case they got the wrong idea. Steven took me into a corner and started to get passionate. He was definitely getting turned on by the whole thing. I snogged him briefly, but I wasn't comfortable at all. And when he tried to put his hand down my trousers I decided I'd had enough and insisted we left straight away.

When Steven had finished regaling me with his sordid goings-on I told him what had happened to me. The look of disbelief on his face grew with everything I said. He wouldn't believe that Mike had any kind of amnesia, accusing him of being 'an ungrateful little shit'. I skipped the part where I wanked Mike off as I thought that would be sharing too much. When I told him about the doctor's reaction he demanded to know who it was. I hadn't noticed his name, but I could give him a pretty good description. He had to be the cutest doctor I'd ever seen. For some reason that made everything clear to Steven. He explained that this particular doctor had been in a violent relationship himself. He didn't manage to get himself out of it until the guy involved did him some serious damage. Now he was very keen to support anyone who might be in a similar situation. He even did a stint with the local gay switchboard. Steven offered to straighten things out, but I said I'd do it myself, now I understood what was going on. All Steven had to do was make sure I got to speak to the doctor without being escorted from the premises by security.

Steven had a few more minutes before his shift started, so he went off to find out what rota the doctor was working and whether he'd be around to cause hassle for me this afternoon if we didn't sort things out. It turned out he was back on duty and Steven managed to get him to agree to see me for a few minutes as long as it was now. He took me up to the duty sister's office on his way to start his shift and wished me luck as he left me there. I promised to let him know how I got on. From the leer he gave me as he left I think he half expected me to get up to something sordid with the handsome doctor while we were alone. I decided to play this one carefully, knocked on the door and waited to be invited in.

Inside the room the doctor was perched on the edge of the desk looking as impressive as ever. He couldn't have had much more sleep than Steven, but it didn't seem to have bothered him. He looked immaculate in his crisp shirt, freshly pressed trousers and white coat. I still couldn't shake the feeling that he was really an actor playing a role rather than a stressed-out medic. His leaning against the edge of the desk may make it sound like the atmosphere was casual, but it was far from it. It's a position which is carefully calculated to give a relaxed impression while causing quite the opposite feeling in the other person. And I was sure he knew it. If I sat down he'd be looking down at me in a superior, possibly patronising position. If I remained standing it was still leaving me in a submissive role. The only way to deal with that is if you know the person well enough to perch on the desk next to them and face each other as equals. I didn't. And his body language made sure I was aware of that. His feet were crossed at the ankles and his arms were folded across his chest. Boy, was I feeling intimidated.

He didn't waste any time in letting me know that I was only there because Steven was a good friend of his and had persuaded him to see me. And that he was on a tight schedule so I'd better get on with it. I decided to work on the common ground between us: Steven. I apologised for being less than completely open when I spoke to him last, but that my situation with Mike was very personal. I was only trying to explain now because Steven had assured me that he wouldn't be judgmental and might even understand. From the look on his face I thought I might have gone too far with the compliments so I pressed on quickly.

I told him I'd met Mike in a club the night before and that we'd gone back to my place. I glossed over any sexual details. I explained that Mike wasn't happy when I'd had to ask him to leave and that's when I'd given him my calling card. I didn't know what had happened to him since then and I had only become involved again because Steven had found my card in Mike's pocket and called me. And I was glad he did because I wanted to do anything I could to help ease Mike's obvious suffering. The doctor's posture unfolded a bit and he asked me why I'd kicked Mike out. I tried to cover a little, saying that I'd unexpectedly found a friend in my room who was in some kind of trouble. That wasn't enough. I suppose it did sound a bit far fetched. I looked into his piercing blue eyes and I couldn't help myself. It all flooded out. The main points of my entire off-and-on relationship with Tim from when I first met him to when he left me without a word this morning. By the time I'd finished I felt totally naked and even more vulnerable.

When I looked up at the doctor again I thought I could see understanding and empathy in his deep, expressive eyes. He'd loosened up completely. His feet were now spread apart and his hands were resting on the desk at his sides. My emotions felt so raw I didn't know whether to cry or hug him or both. I didn't get the chance.

He glanced at his watch and said he had to go. He also told me that he'd seen what I'd done to cheer up Mike's room and spoken to the nurse who had helped me. That was partly why he'd agreed to see me, but it could have still been the actions of a guilty party, especially when I'd seemed to be covering something up when we first spoke. Now he apologised for his previous actions and hoped I would understand it had been the end of a deeply stressful shift and he had been concerned for the welfare of his patient. I took the hand he offered me and went weak at the knees when he shook it in a firm grip. I wondered if all his patients fell in love with him and how quickly I could get him away from Mike, just to be on the safe side. He said he really did have to get on and I realised I was still holding his hand. Blushing slightly I let him guide me to the door and tried to think of a way to get to see him again. When I suggested that both he and Steven come round for a meal sometime he just smiled and said 'perhaps' as he left me by the door to Mike's room.

I looked through the window and saw Steven in there with Mike. They seemed to be arguing, and from the look of the pile of things on Mike's lap it was getting nasty. I was on the verge of bursting in to break things up when Steven noticed me looking through the window. He fired another verbal shot that seemed to be the telling blow. Mike sort of went limp as if conceding defeat and Steven headed to the door. Pushing me into the room he just muttered, 'Don't blow it now' and left us to it.

I hadn't a clue what had happened and didn't know what to do next. I asked Mike how he was feeling and started to clear away the things from his lap. I really couldn't figure it out. It was all the stuff I'd brought for him. I just tidied them away in his locker and asked if I could do anything else. When he asked me to explain what had happened last night, I just couldn't help myself. Once again I found myself revealing my life story to a relative stranger. People say I'm too open, but that's just the way I am. I didn't hold anything back, right up to Tim leaving without even saying goodbye. Now I really was feeling emotional. I can't quite remember what happened next, but I know Mike said he was feeling tired and I was about to leave him to get some rest when Steven burst back into the room.

Now I don't know what had rattled his cage, but he was definitely out for blood this time. He just laid into Mike telling him he was going to be moved onto a main ward and making it sound like Hell on Earth. He batted away all Mike's feeble attempts to protest with utter contempt until it looked as if he had no choice in the matter. It seemed he couldn't go home because he had to be looked after and he lived alone. That's when I decided he could stay with me. For some reason Steven didn't approve of the idea, but Mike jumped at the chance so it was all settled.

Steven stormed out of the room again. I felt as if things were finally starting to get resolved. Mike would be out of this place and have someone to look after him. I'd be making up for kicking him out and so being partly responsible for whatever had happened to him. And you never know what might happen when we got to know each other better. Mike said he really was feeling tired now, so I left him alone to get some rest. I found Steven at reception and asked what was going on. He didn't want to talk about it just saying that I could come and 'get him off their hands' later that evening. Whatever had got to Steven, I figured he was better left to work it out by himself so I headed for home to get things sorted out. I had a lot of work to do before the spare room was habitable.

I had that dream again. The one where I'm running through the forest but don't know why. As before, I just knew I had to keep running, and the forest was very dark and dense and I kept stumbling over tree roots. I was panting for breath and my legs were turning to rubber, but I knew I couldn't stop or something terrible would happen. The forest was getting denser and branches kept whipping across me. I had to slow to a walk to force my way through the foliage. I was scratched and sore, but just like before I couldn't stop until I heard someone cry out and then when I looked for them there was nothing there, literally, and I found myself stood at the edge of a cliff. Again I swayed precariously and took a half step back to regain my balance. Again I heard the second cry for help, coming from beneath me, and I looked down at my feet to find pair of hands clinging to the edge of the cliff. Again it was Tim, hanging on like grim death, looking up at me with those beautiful eyes of his pleading with me to help him. But then the dream changed.

I was about to drop to the ground to help when I heard another cry for help to my left. I looked across and there was another pair of hands clinging to the cliff edge. I looked over the edge and there was Mike hanging on like grim death, and he looked up at me with his beautiful eyes pleading with me to help him. I didn't know what to do. I couldn't reach them both. It wasn't fair being forced to choose between them.

Then I heard voices behind me. I turned and saw Steven and the doctor standing there arm in arm, looking at me with disgust. 'Well, don't just stand there. Do something,' they prompted in unison. I just stared at them helplessly. 'Too late,' they said. And I heard two separate cries from behind me as both Tim and Mike fell into the bottomless abyss.

I rushed to the edge and peered over, hoping they might have found something else to grab onto before falling too far. I couldn't see anything down there. Suddenly I felt the ground beneath me start to crumble. Struggling to keep my balance, I turned to the others for help. I just saw Steven and the doctor turn and start to walk away. I called out as I slipped over the edge and scrabbled for a grip in the loose soil. Nobody heard me and I found myself falling. Falling into the bottomless abyss.

As I fell I managed to grab hold of a ledge. I started to pull myself painfully up to safety when I heard voices above me. I could just see over the edge and there were Tim and Mike having sex together. Then I felt the ledge start to crumble in my hands. I called out as I scrabbled for a grip in the loose soil. Either they didn't hear me or they didn't care because they just carried on as I found myself falling again. And I knew that this time I wasn't going to stop.

I woke up with a start, feeling totally disoriented. At first I thought the cries I could hear were just remnants of the dream. Then I remembered Mike in the spare room. Maybe he was in trouble. I jumped out of bed and rushed to his room. In the little light that came from the open door I could see that he was still asleep. He must have been having a nightmare as well. With another cry Mike woke up and tried to sit up before he remembered his bandages and casts. The room was still dark, so I was careful walking across to the bed. I knew how much clutter there was in there and it wouldn't be any good if I fell over something and we were both out of action. When I reached Mike's side I sat on the edge of the bed and took him in my arms. I could think of no other way to comfort him, so I hugged him to me and gently kissed his bruised lips. Briefly my mind flashed on the sight of him having sex with Tim in my dream. Now that I wasn't fighting for my life I realised what a horny image that was and my cock sprang to life. Well, there would be plenty of time for that later. After all, Mike wasn't going anywhere for some time. I just settled down on the bed next to him and snuggled up against his warm body.

Chapter Twenty-one

MIKE

When I come to I remember nothing. I know it sounds clichéd, but it's true. I do recognise the feeling, though. I've had a hypo. I guess I should be more careful about checking my sugar levels, but I just don't want it to take over my life. It always takes a while for me to come round properly after a hypo, and some memories just don't come back at all. Mind you, in my line of work there are some memories I'm glad to be rid of. Anyway, I'm not surprised when I can't move at first. The old muscles take a while to recover as well. I just try to keep still and let my mind wander to try to remember what I can. At the moment all I'm getting are vague emotions. There's frustration, anger, horniness (nothing new there) and behind it all an unhealthy dose of fear. I just keep getting a flash of an evil grin. Have I been attacked by the Cheshire cat? Then I become aware of a fuss going on around me. I figure it's time to face the world and slowly prise one eye open. I slam it shut quickly trying to deny the reality of what I see. The memories of earlier in the evening come flooding back. What the fuck is he doing here?

Maybe if I keep my eyes closed he'll think I've slipped back into a coma and just piss off. No such luck. He's got hold of my shoulder and he's shaking it with enough force to rattle every aching bone in my body. But then, why are the bones in my body aching? I still can't remember what happened just before I blacked out. Now there's another voice calling to me from my other side. I figure I've no choice but to admit I'm awake and open my eyes. I still wish I hadn't.

I had planned to play the poor defenceless soul (you know, gaze through anguished eyes and mutter helplessly, 'Where am I?') but when I realise the state I'm in, I can't stop my natural response. I try to sit bolt upright, shouting 'What the fuck . . . ?' Despite my best efforts I just collapse back onto the bed. A hospital bed. A bed in a hospital! Eventually I realise why I can't sit up. My arms are in plaster and there's a tight bandage around my chest, all of which has totally screwed my balance. There's a nurse at the side of my bed (I'm still trying not to look at him over there) and she tries to calm me down. In that soothing voice you use for little kids and senile pensioners she tells me I should keep still because I'm in a bad way (like I don't already know) and that there'll be a doctor here soon (like that'll make everything okay). I decide to play along for now. Besides, I hurt too much to do anything else.

The nurse checks my pulse – she has to feel my throat as my wrists are covered in the plaster – and then she really does the dirty on me. She walks out and leaves me alone with *him*. I consider trying to feign a relapse, but he'd probably panic and shout for emergency treatment. I decide to try ignoring him and stare pointedly at the window where the nurse had been stood. He's prattling on, asking how I am and other such garbage. He's obviously not going to give up so I try another tack. I slowly turn my head toward him, keeping my expression blank and mumble, 'Who are you?' He looks mildly surprised for a moment and then introduces himself, saying that we'd met at a club last night. Then he starts banging on about how much pain I must be in because I look terrible. I'm still playing dumb, but wondering how much I'd hurt if I clock him with a plaster cast, when he's rescued by the doctor's entrance.

Now, I don't normally go for the Doctor Kildare type, but this guy's quite cute. And besides he's a regular knight in shining armour. He ushers Colin (yes, I remembered his name, but I wasn't telling him that) out of the room, saying he wants to examine me in private. I wish! When he comes back he shines a light in my eyes and says he's checking for concussion. Apparently I haven't got one. He also says I've got some mild fractures in my arms, some bruising to my ribs and a mild surface wound on my head. All the while he's pressing his hands all over my body asking where it hurts. If he goes any lower he's likely to find out 'cause suddenly my cock's coming to life. Now I remember where the feeling of frustration fits in. Colin at the club, the porn mag at his flat, the guy at the service station. I never did get my end away. My libido's been up and down all night without any satisfaction. At least that explains the ache in my balls. I was worried I might have been damaged down there too.

Anyway, the doctor seems satisfied and tells me that the damage is all superficial and that I should be able to go home in a few days. He flashes a brilliant smile and asks if there's anything he can do to make me more comfortable. I'm about to risk telling him when I notice Colin peering through the glass in the door. 'You could keep him away from me,' I say. The doctor looks surprised and asks why, and has he got anything to do with the state I'm in. It's too easy, so I just say, 'Yeah, it's all his fault.' Well, technically it was. If he hadn't thrown me out I wouldn't have been in the service station in the first place. Then none of this would have happened. The doctor gives me a funny look for a moment, then walks out. At the door I see him guiding Colin away. 'At least I'm rid of him,' I think as I slip into a drug-induced sleep.

I don't know if it's a guilty conscience or the drugs, but I have this weird dream. Or maybe it really happened and I'm still a bit mixed up after the hypo? Anyway, I'm in this really deep sleep when my memory starts to fill in a few more blanks. I'm in the loo at the service station and there's a riot going on outside the cubicle. Of course I'm totally naked. There's this other guy in there with me, but he's shaking in a corner. Suddenly these hands start to break through the cubicle walls. No, they aren't breaking through. They're just passing through the wood like ghosts. Once through the wall they're solid, though, and I find myself trapped by them. The hands are all over me, holding me tight. My arms and legs are spread wide and there's another hand clutching at my groin. It rubs firmly at my crotch and I'm getting an erection. Then another hand grabs my hair and pulls my head up. The cubicle door slams open and a bank of fog comes rolling in. The other guy turns into a huge rabbit and hops away. A dark figure looms in the doorway. It fairly glides across the cubicle until its face is right up against mine. I recognise the face. I don't know who it belongs to, but I know I've seen it before. Maybe it's the expression I recognise. It's a mixture of superiority and loathing. I try to pull free, but the hands hold fast. I'm scared, but I'm also excited. The face asks me what I want. I can't quite place the voice. It seems to come from far away even though the face is right against mine. I muster my courage and cry, 'I want a wank!' as defiantly as I can. The face grins. The hand at my groin is going into overdrive gliding up and down my cock. The face sneers at me. I feel a sharp point pressing against my ribs. The face smiles at me. It doesn't say anything, but it really doesn't have to. That smile is pure evil. The pressure at my chest gets tighter. My cock is throbbing. As the point pierces my chest one of the hands finds my arse and a finger slides into my hole. The face is laughing hysterically as I lose it and come spurts from my cock as blood spurts from my chest.

I wake up with a start and realise I'm not alone. The room's in darkness, but I can feel this presence hovering above the bed. I can't come round fully, but I can feel the dampness at my groin being mopped up with some sort of tissue before I slip back into darkness.

I'm finally woken by light shining onto my face. I force my eyes to open and see a blurred outline against the brightness of the window. 'Good afternoon,' it says, far too cheerfully. 'I hope you slept well.' The figure comes into focus as it moves toward the bed. It's a guy with a clipboard. 'Now, I'm going to need some details from you. Starting with your name.' I'm not properly awake and so I give him my details before stopping to consider whether it would have been better to lie.

'And just what happened to you last night?' he asks next. I tell him I don't remember. It's still true. I don't remember anything after the guy threatening me in the loos.

'So what have you got against Colin?'

'Pardon?'

'Oh, cut the crap. We both know he couldn't have done this to you.'

I'm too stunned to say anything for a while. 'I didn't say he did,' I venture while I try to work out what to do next. But I can't hear myself think, the way the guy keeps going on at me.

'You gave the doctor the impression he was involved. He was all set to call the police in and have Colin charged. But I don't think you'd want the police to get too involved, would you? You never know what else they might find out about.'

Now, I don't take kindly to threats. Especially from jumped-up clerks I've never met before. But before I get the chance to work on a suitable reply he's at it again.

'Colin doesn't deserve that kind of treatment. He's been really good to you. Where do you think all these flowers came from?'

Now I was feeling petulant. 'I have hay fever.'

'And the chocolates?'

'Duh, I'm diabetic, remember? What's he trying to do? Kill me?'

'If you bothered to look, you'd see they're specially for diabetics.'

'Yeah, and you know the sugar-substitute in them acts as a laxative in certain quantities. If I ate that lot I'd be permanently stuck to a bedpan.'

'And there's all these magazines.' He drops a pile on the bed. I'm sure he'd aimed deliberately to land them on my groin.

'I can't turn the pages in these casts, can I?'

'Maybe not, but I'm sure he'd even read them to you. And he's left this.' He opens my locker and drops a personal stereo onto the pile of magazines in my lap. 'And these.' A selection of tapes join the heap. 'And even these.' Spare batteries are next. I can tell I'm losing this one. Colin had thought of everything.

'So the guy's a saint.' I say. 'What d'you expect me to do about it? I didn't ask for any of this.'

'Maybe you didn't. And you don't deserve it. He's too good for the likes of you. But for some reason he's taken to you and you're his latest crusade, so the least you can do is be grateful.'

'He can't buy my gratitude.'

'It's not just these. He's even more considerate than that. He's been here all the time you were sleeping. The only time he left your side was when he went to get these things. Even after you had him kicked out, he stayed outside the door in case he could do anything. He's still there now.'

'Yeah, well, he wasn't so nice last night.'

'I don't know what went down between you two last night, but knowing Colin I'm sure there was a damn good reason for whatever it was. I figure you should at least see him and hear him out. I think you owe him that.'

Maybe I'm going soft in my old age. Or maybe it's been too long since anyone was so considerate. Either way, I give in and the guy pushes Colin into the room and then disappears, leaving us to it.

Now, Colin is much less forceful. He looks really nervous, in fact. While we're talking he starts tidying the pile of things from my lap and putting them away neatly in my locker. He just asks how I'm feeling and if there's anything he can do. I tell him I think he's done more than enough, but he looks so dejected I finally ask him to explain about last night. I get the whole tale. More than I need, in fact. The sob story about his ex-lover. The entire history between them. This guy is really fixated. Then he tells me how his ex had turned up out of the blue last night, which was why he'd kicked me out. How he'd tried to comfort him. How they'd ended up having sex. Somehow it always boils down to sex, doesn't it? Next comes the part where he's feeling used because the guy didn't stay for breakfast. I tell him that's the way life works and he's probably better off without him. He gives me such a look. I've never seen such raw emotion in one pair of eyes before. I can feel myself starting to melt and I don't want that. I tell him I'm feeling tired so perhaps he should go and I almost succeed when the clipboard guy bustles back into the room.

'Don't go getting too comfortable,' he says. 'You're being moved soon.' Colin looks as surprised by this one as I am.

'Where to?' I ask.

'Onto the main ward. You were only put in this side room because you were unconscious and we needed to keep an eye on you. Now you've been examined properly, you've been pronounced fit to join everyone else. We need the room, anyway. We're so short of beds at the moment that we'll have to put you on the geriatric ward. But I'm sure you'll soon make new friends there.'

This worries me. 'I don't want to spend my time stuck like this with a bunch of drooling old farts,' I tell him.

'I thought you'd be used to it by now. Anyway, it's not like you have a choice.'

'Why can't I go home?'

'Because you live on your own and you need someone to look after you for a while. At least until those casts come off.'

'I have friends who'll keep an eye out for me.'

'Then why aren't they here visiting? You've not asked for anyone to be contacted. And you didn't give me a next of kin when I was taking your details.'

It looks as if he's won again. I wouldn't be surprised if the vicious old queen had engineered this move deliberately to spite me.

'He can stay with me,' says Colin forcefully. 'You know I'll look after him.' The clerk's face is a picture. I don't know what's gone on between those two, but he obviously isn't taken with the suggestion. It looks like I'm low on choices and I'd love to get one over on that guy, so I find myself agreeing with Colin. Maybe he's not such a bad sort after all.

The clerk storms off in a huff, muttering something about it all being highly irregular. Colin looks as if he's just won the lottery. I've never seen anyone look so happy without having an orgasm. Now I tell him I really am feeling tired, so he leaves as well, saying he's got things to sort out.

I'm having that dream again. I know it's a dream, but that doesn't make it any better. I'm back in the loo at the service station and there's the riot going on outside the cubicle. Of course I'm still totally naked. There's the other guy in there with me shaking in a corner. Suddenly the hands pass through the cubicle walls like ghosts. Once through the wall they're solid and I find myself trapped by them again. Just like before, the hands are all over me, holding me tight. My arms and legs are spread wide and there's another hand clutching at my groin. It rubs firmly at my crotch and I'm getting an erection. Then another hand grabs my hair and pulls my head up. The cubicle door slams open and a bank of fog comes rolling in. The other guy turns into a huge rabbit and hops away. The dark figure looms in the doorway, then glides across the cubicle until its face is right up against mine. I still recognise the face. I don't know who it belongs to, but I know I've seen it before. It's the ringleader of the gang who attacked me at the service station. His expression is a mixture of superiority and loathing. I try to pull free, but the hands hold fast. I'm scared, but I'm also excited. The face doesn't speak. It just grins. The hand at my groin is going into overdrive, gliding up and down my cock. The face sneers at me. I feel a sharp point pressing against my ribs. The face smiles at me. It still doesn't say anything, but it really doesn't have to. That smile is pure evil. The pressure at my chest gets tighter. My cock is throbbing. As the point begins to pierce my chest, the cubicle door slams open again. This time there's a shining light bursting through the fog. A glistening figure makes its way through the light and stands impressively in the doorway. The face screams in terror and crumbles into dust. The hands vanish and I'm suddenly free. I turn to face my knight in shining armour as he removes his helmet. Colin looks back at me with that look of ecstatic happiness.

I wake up with a start and for a moment I don't know where I am. Then I remember. I'm in bed in Colin's spare room. I realise I'm not alone. The room's in darkness, but I can feel this presence hovering somewhere. I look around and see Colin stood in the open doorway. I must have called out in my sleep. I can feel the sweat soaking my whole body. Colin cautiously crosses the room to the bed and embraces me. He gently kisses my bruised lips and my groin begins to stir. What have I let myself in for?

EPILOGUE

It has been said that time is a great healer, but will the mental scars of the past twenty-four hours remain with our friends after the physical wounds have gone?

Mike's happy to stay with Colin now while he needs to be looked after, but how will he feel when Colin tries to continue looking after him when he is able to fend for himself? Will they grow closer together, as Colin hopes? How will Colin cope with Mike's occupation if he finds out about it? Perhaps Mike will try to make a fresh start with him instead of returning to it. What will he do for money then? And what might happen at the dinner party that Colin's planning to throw to celebrate Mike's recovery? Will Steven and Doctor Charles regret accepting their invitations?

Will Tim get the chance to make another go of his relationship with Pete? Or will it fall apart under the strain of Pete's new found taste for excitement? Will Pete make it up to Rick so they can carry on fooling around? If so, will Tim find out about it or will he carry on deluding himself?

And what about our 'straight' friends? Will they carry on abusing people or will they get their come-uppance? Or will they find another outlet for their aggression? One where they can treat people who are into that sort of thing as rough as they like for mutual satisfaction. Or would they still go too far?

The word is that there's a new club opening in town. One where people are free to explore their darker passions and are guaranteed satisfaction. It sounds like just the sort of place where Mike and Colin can stretch the boundaries of their fledgling relationship; where Pete can sample the excitement he now craves; where Rick can discover whether he's really into being abused; where Steven can pass the time between shifts. A place where the Kid can get a job to help him find the money and self-respect to keep him off the streets, and where Mack and Carl will feel right at home.

Or is it?